'It's a wonder he could do his job.' Sasha felt helpless. 'I was the one who recognised his change of personality. It's my fault completely. If he dies—'

Adam said quickly, 'Wait till we do all the tests. No point in getting emotional.'

'It's all right for you—' Sasha stopped herself. 'I'm sorry.' They faced each other across Adam's desk, the photograph of Joe's tumour between them. It seemed symbolic—Joe's illness had brought Sasha back to him. Her loyalty and her guilt feelings would see to that. She faced Adam and couldn't think of anything to say. 'I'm sorry,' she repeated.

Adam said quietly, 'You mustn't go back to him if you aren't in live with him.'

'That's not important. He needs me.'

'You can't live a lie.'

'There's nothing else to do.'

'But there has to be!'

Lancashire born, Jenny Ashe read English at Birmingham, returning thence with a BA and RA—the latter being rheumatoid arthritis, which after barrels of various pills, and three operations, led to her becoming almost bionic, with two man-made joints. Married to a junior surgeon in Scotland, who was born in Malaysia, she returned to Liverpool with three Scottish children when her husband went into general practice in 1966. She has written non-stop since then—articles, short stories and radio talks. Her novels just had to be set in a medical environment, which she considers compassionate, fascinating and completely rewarding.

Previous Titles
SISTER HARRIET'S HEART
DOCTOR RORY'S RETURN
THE SURGEON FROM SAN AGUSTIN
SISTER AT GREYRIGG

MISPLACED LOYALTY

BY

JENNY ASHE

MILLS & BOON LIMITED
ETON HOUSE   18-24 PARADISE ROAD
RICHMOND   SURREY   TW9 1SR

First published in Great Britain 1989
by Mills & Boon Limited

© Jenny Ashe 1989

Australian copyright 1989
Philippine copyright 1989
This edition 1989

ISBN 0 263 76510 5

Set in English Times 10 on 10 pt.
03 – 8908 – 53200

Typeset in Great Britain by JCL Graphics, Bristol

Made and Printed in Great Britain

CHAPTER ONE

THE drab Liverpool hospital smelt of damp and unwashed people. It was Saturday night, and the waiting-room in Casualty was full. The gaudy plastic chairs were stained with blood, old urine, grimy hands and discarded chewing-gum, and the muddied tiles were constantly tramped over by blank and disconsolate humanity. The receptionists were swamped with moans and cries in varying degrees of desperation, and a dishevelled Sister McKeown fought her way through the crowd to try to weed out the more urgent cases for the doctors to see first.

'Sister, I was discharged yesterday and me wound's opened up!'

'Sister, this woman over 'ere's 'aemorrhagin'—d'yer want 'er ter bleed ter death?'

'Sister, the doctor wants his tea!'

'Sister, wure do ah go, luv, with me 'ip?'

Dr Sasha Norton sympathised with them all, especially Carrie McKeown. Sasha was coming to the end of her stint as casualty officer, and would soon be free of this constant strain and endless workload. Carrie was stuck here for good. Sasha worked without fuss, closing her ears to the noise, examining, stitching, taking blood and giving injections. She heard her consultant, Dr Mortimer, again asking if there was any tea. He had come in specially tonight to give Sasha a hand as they were so busy, and the least he expected for his pains was a cup of decent tea. The rain beat on the glass doors and the constant stream of patients trod mud and filth into the floor.

'Sister—send this patient to Dr Norton—he only needs a couple of stitches. And, in the name of all the

5

archangels, find me some tea!' Philip Mortimer
appeared to be getting towards the end of his tether
without tea, and was sending her more work—and she
knew why. She had refused to go back with him after
the party on Friday. And Philip Mortimer thought no
one could refuse him. He was a good doctor, but he
suffered from being single because nice girls distrusted
his Porsche and his flashy life-style.

'It's OK, Carrie—I don't mind. Wheel him in.' Sasha
waited for the boy with the gashed forehead to be
wheeled in in a chair. The nurse who brought him was
just about to leave when Sasha said, 'Don't you dare go
and put the kettle on, Nurse. I'll need you here. I'm
running out of sutures.'

'OK, Doctor, but he'll be hopping mad!'

'Tell him I needed you.' Sasha coolly mopped at the
gash that was still spurting blood. 'Let him shout at me
instead of you. I'm leaving soon—I can take it.' She
smiled briefly at the young student nurse. 'Would you
mind swabbing here, please?' And, as the two women
worked, the crowd of wet, miserable people kept
growing, so that the queue spilled out into the corridor.

'Nurse! Where the devil are you?' Sasha had almost
finished her stitches, so she nodded to the frightened
girl, and gave her an encouraging wink as she scurried
off towards the office. Sasha tied the knot and snipped
the last suture with small scissors. It wasn't the patients'
fault that there were not enough staff or facilities. Sasha
found it easy to cope, as long as they didn't get stroppy.
But when an old man was wheeled in with an obvious
fracture of his neck of femur, it was hard to control
certain sections of the waiting-room, who saw him
getting immediate attention from the casualty officer.
Liverpool people were not slow to demand their rights,
and Sasha sighed, wishing they could do so a little more
quietly.

'He's lying down! Warrabout us? Been 'ere since nine
o'clock!'

Sasha turned and looked at them, trying not to quail.

Her white coat gave her authority, and she was quite tall, with wide brown eyes and straight brown hair that hung behind her ears. 'I'm sorry, but this is an emergency.' She tried to make her usually quiet voice sharp and authoritative. 'Get him straight to X-ray.' The nurses and the porters knew the drill anyway. It was to keep the waiting crowds quiet that she raised her voice.

As the trolley was being wheeled away, Sasha noticed a trickle of blood from the old man's ear. 'Wait—let me just take a look at him. Was anyone with him when he fell? I'd better just test his nervous system.' He was brought behind the curtain, and she examined him more thoroughly.

'He was alone, Doctor. A neighbour sent for the ambulance—when she found him on the floor when she took his shopping in.'

Sasha took out her tendon hammer. 'In that case, I believe he may have collapsed *before* breaking the bone.' She checked his reflexes carefully. Then she checked his eyes, which were half-closed. Yes, she was right. One eye was definitely not focusing. 'I'd better phone for the neuro registrar. Perhaps they can arrange for X-ray when he's seen him.' She went to the phone. 'Neuro, please. Dr Moore.'

'Harrington here.'

It was the big man himself. How come he was answering his own phone? Sasha had only seen him in passing, and assumed that he would be scathing and superior like most consultants to their juniors. Yet his voice sounded almost reasonable. She began to apologise. 'Oh, Mr Harrington, I didn't mean—I mean, it's Dr Norton here, AED. I just wanted Pat Moore to take a look at a seventy-year-old man who's just been brought in with a query neck of femur. I think it's a CVA.'

'Pat's busy in the ward, Dr Norton. I'll pop down and take a look.'

Sasha wasn't sure how senior consultants reacted

when sent for by Casualty. Adam Harrington sounded almost human. But she had known some who never had a civil word for the doctor who summoned them. True, they were usually in a tearing hurry anyway. She turned back to the patient. There wasn't a nurse in sight, and his blood pressure seemed very low.

There was no time to hang about waiting for Mr Harrington. Sasha had the stroke patient wheeled to one side, while she waited for the next patient. Carrie charged in with all the finesse of a bull elephant. 'Doc, another heart attack! We've no beds left, and no trolleys!'

'I'll come and see him.' Sasha hurried to the pale, sweating figure on the ambulance trolley. She took his pulse carefully and listened to his heart. The ambulance staff were wanting their trolley back. Sasha looked up. 'Can't we put a mattress down there, Sister? He'll need ECG at once, of course. Can you find a free monitor?'

Sister said, 'Don't you think we should send him to the Royal?'

Sasha shook her head. 'No. No time. Find him a mattress or something, Sister, and supervise the ECG. Here, let's give him something for the pain.' She was handed the usual ten milligrams of Diomorphine. With practised fingers she broke the phial of distilled water, and injected the drug intravenously. 'Keep an eye on him, Sister—I've got to get back to my CVA. Mr Harrington's coming down to see him.'

Carrie raised her eyebrows at the other side of the prostrate patient. 'Adam Harrington? Why? Is the patient someone important?'

'Don't think so. Harrington took the phone when I rang the department, that's all. I asked for the registrar, but Harrington said he'd pop down.'

Sister grinned, her cheerful red face always ready to do so. 'Well, it's our lucky day. Mr Harrington can come down and scrub my back any day! He's a duck, is Mr Harrington.' And she bustled away to see about the ECG, and deal with yet another fracas in the queue with good humour.

A man was standing with hands on hips. 'I've bin 'ere since nine this morning. What the hell do you lot think you're playin' at behind them curtains?'

Just then the woman who had been haemorrhaging passed out, sliding to the floor with a little moan. Sasha snapped, 'Get her to Gynae at once!' Philip should have seen to it. Was this another of his cases he was leaving for her?

Philip came out looking harassed. 'You mean the Gynae houseman didn't come and see when I rang him?' He cursed under his breath, and waited until the patient was taken up to the ward.

The man who was complaining strode forward. 'Here, I want a word with you. Let me tell you, I'm a councillor, and the state of this department is going to be reported to my MP. I've bin 'ere since this morning. I left a council meeting to come 'ere.'

A small man at the back of the queue shouted, 'Wharr 'appened, mate? Too much brandy, was it?'

The councillor turned round, his eyes bulging, his face turning purple. 'Who said that?' The words possibly hit a raw nerve. But there was no time for retribution, as the scream of an approaching siren heralded the arrival of another patient.

'Heart attack in the pub. Get the doc, quick!' But Sasha had already pressed the alert button. Carrie found more screens from somewhere, and the casualty was curtained off and Sasha went to see to him as the arrest trolley was wheeled round for her. Philip came in.

'I'll do this one.' His voice was quiet. Possibly he saw from her face how tired she was feeling.

She left that cubicle to go back to her own. The councillor called out to her, but she adopted a look of being preoccupied with some great philosophical concept and edged past him without a word. There was a sudden loud crash of glass that stilled the general hubbub. Sasha looked at the main door with a sigh, an expression of irritation on her face. Vandals again. Four smallish lads saw her coming, and dashed away into the wet car park with harsh screams of raucous laughter. At least they hadn't broken the glass to the receptionist's office. This time it was only an empty lemonade bottle smashed right in the main doorway, where it could cause most mayhem and distress. Already a small girl had picked up a piece of glass, and her fingers were bleeding.

'Tetanus!' Sasha had picked her up and taken her into the cubicle. She cleaned the wound, bandaged it, and injected the anti-tetanus serum. Around her the maintenance team swept up the glass and made sure there were no shattered fragments among the wet filth outside the door. At least that left the place slightly more hygienic. The girl's mother had come with a sprained ankle, and was annoyed when she was sent back to the waiting-room to wait her turn. The girl was crying now, with the pain of the cut hand and the injection.

Sasha ran back to where she had left her stroke victim. As she had though, Mr Harrington was already there, examining him. He was speaking to the patient in a quiet, calm voice, as though nothing else was happening at all around him. He looked up at Sasha and she recognised the gentle grey eyes, the hair silvering at the temples, the intelligent forehead and dark brows of the senior neuro-surgeon whom she had only seen before at a distance. 'Hello, Doctor. You were quite right to call me—it is a stroke. Sister, will you arrange for this man and his notes to be transferred to Nelson Ward?' Sister had materialised in time, and she called a porter to take the patient. Harrington said, 'I'll arrange for his hip to be seen in the ward.'

'Thank you very much.'

'That's all right. How do you manage to stay sane down here?'

'I'm not sure that we do, sir.'

He was smiling, seemingly in no hurry to leave, when the junior nurse came in in tears. At the sight of the consultant she ran out again. Adam Harrington said, 'I suppose you can diagnose what the tears are for?'

'I think so. Dr Mortimer hasn't had any tea.'

'Oh, dear.' They exchanged another smile. Then he said, 'I see my man is on the way up. I'll go and see that he sees the orthopods tonight.' She thanked him again, feeling how he created an island of serenity around him. He said, 'By the way, it's Dr Norton, isn't it? What's your first name?'

'Sasha.'

He held out his hand. 'Glad to meet you, Dr Sasha Norton.' And, with a twinkle in his grey eyes, he was gone, leaving her staring after him.

What a pleasant, handsome, reasonable man. He had civilised Casualty for one short moment. Sasha smoothed her hair back, with an unaccountable wish that she had looked a little more tidy for her first meeting with Adam Harrington.

Sister came in. 'We can't ward the heart attack.'

'Why ever not?'

'No beds.'

'What rubbish. We're a hospital, aren't we? Get me Dr Low on the phone.' Sasha was a mild girl, but she had learned from bitter experience at the Liverpool Western Hospital that a junior doctor got nowhere unless she shouted louder than the others. She used her best head-girl voice. 'Doctor, I've one confirmed heart attack, and another just come in. Will you please come down and confirm that they require immediate coronary care?'

'OK, Sasha, don't get your knickers in a twist. I'll do what I can.'

'Good for you, Chris.' They were really good friends, but they both had to cope with inadequate back-up. 'Make it snappy.' She went back to the second coronary case. 'Did the injection help? We'll be sending you to the coronary ward soon—Dr Low will be looking after you.'

The man said through white lips, 'I don't know how you do it, luv.' She smiled, very aware that most

patients were grateful, nice people. There was a very
loud, blood-curdling scream from the waiting area.
Sasha turned.

The nurse popped her head round. 'It's that loony
from Beckwith Street.'

Sister came in. 'I'll see to him, Doctor. He only wants
someone to take a bit of notice of him—one of the
regulars, with a nice fat file, but he'll go home if I give
him a smile and a cup of tea.'

Sasha said drily, 'Then don't forget to give Dr
Mortimer a cup while the kettle's on.' She looked
outside. The lights were all on in the corridors, the dank
car park lit up, its puddles shining in the lamplight.

Philip Mortimer appeared. 'You still here, Sasha? It's
an hour past your knock-off time. Get out of here,
woman, and don't come back.' He had clearly forgiven
her for the snub last night. 'What I want to know is,' he
added, 'why did no one else come on duty?'

'It's the medical houseman, I think. He *is* in the ward,
but you're to call him if you need him.'

'If we need him?' Philip's eyebrows disappeared into
his hair. 'Call him, Sister, call him at once. Dr Norton
will be passing out herself unless she gets out of this
lousy department before midnight.'

She walked across the car park. It was drizzling, and
the tops of the cars reflected the orange lights. There
wasn't much traffic in Western Road, with its Victorian
houses now all made into flats for students and young
people on the dole who had their rent paid for them. A
baby cried briefly, and Sasha looked up at a tiny attic,
where nappies could be seen on a makeshift line. Above
the attic were the ornate tiles of the gabled roofs, which
belonged to a more affluent era, and, above them, a
bleak northern moon. She pushed her hands deeper into
the pockets of her grubby white coat, and walked more
quickly towards the cold square of light that was the
entrance to the doctors' residences. In the bare brick
porch was scrawled, 'Kev rules OK' and 'Mandy luvs
Steve.'

The phone was ringing as she opened her own cheap, blank door. 'Hello?'

'Hello, love. Shattered as usual, are we?'

'Hello, Joe. I'm just this minute in.'

'It's Saturday. Come down to the Everyman for a drink.'

'I'll try.' She kicked off her shoes. Joe was nice. They'd been out for drinks, meals and the odd game of tennis since student days. Sasha smothered a yawn. 'If I don't fall asleep.' In the distance she heard the siren of yet another ambulance. Yes, it did seem like a good idea to go into town to get away from the Western for an hour or two.

She ran a bath and thought about Joe Acourt. He was chief physio, and marvellous with stroke people and sports injuries. He had been so nice and dependable last year, when she'd been a raw houseman, tentative and unsure of herself. He'd been a good friend to have last year. But now . . . she was never sure what mood he would be in. She didn't want to stop seeing him. Yet things weren't as much fun with Joe as they used to be. Sasha lifted the flannel, letting the warm drops pour on to her stomach, and wondered what Adam Harrington was doing at that moment. The nurses gossiped about most of the doctors, but they didn't say much about him—except admire his good looks, his youthful verve as the youngest consultant in the place. His voice—that was lovely, too, sort of low and unruffled and competent. As though one could take all the troubles in the world to him, and he would quietly and calmly sort them out. She turned on the hot tap with her toe. Adam Harrington was too aloof, too far out of her sphere, for her even to guess what he was doing. Certainly not lying in a chipped bath, planning to find something sensational to wear to go to the Everyman Theatre bar for a drink.

She was just passing the door of the flat below when she heard a muffled noise inside. Surely young houseman Barbara Green should be on the wards tonight? She knocked briskly on the door, and, after a minute or two, it opened to reveal Barbara in a towelling robe, her hair dishevelled and her face streaked with tears. 'Come on in, Sasha. You can be the first to know. I'm leaving. I've had enough.'

Sasha closed the door quickly behind her. 'Barbie, you mean you haven't been to the ward tonight?'

'I'm never going there again. I was up all last night, and I haven't slept today because of the traffic and the ambulances and noise at AED. I'm in no fit state to look after sick people. I just don't care about sick people! I'm better off out of this, and the sooner the better.' Her voice was high and full of self-pity. There was no disguising the fact that she was in a bad state of mind, and her eyes betrayed her lack of sleep.

'Wait here. What you urgently need is a hot mug of tea with two sugars. I don't care if you *are* watching your waistline, you get the sugar and you also get a nice friendly ear to complain into.' She bustled, because she knew it would be dangerous to sympathise too much.

'I wish I knew how to stay cheerful like you.'

Sasha lit the gas and turned round. 'Well, for a start, I had enough sleep last night. I'm also off duty. That makes me cheerful. And my day has been comparatively civilised——'

'How can you possibly say that about Casualty?'

'Well, Philip Mortimer wasn't as dreadful as I expected today, Sister McKeown was positively radiant because Adam Harrington came down to see one of our patients with a cerebrovascular accident, and he actually said "Well done" to us for spotting it.' Sasha made the tea and washed up a couple of dirty mugs that had been left in the sink. 'Not bad, eh? Made everyone's day, that did.' She poured the tea. 'You really are depressed, Barbie. Have you taken anything to help you sleep?'

'I've had two Valium.'

'Better go and see Dr Slade. He's very understanding about housemen's problems—I think he's writing a paper about what stresses they go through.'

'Huh. Isn't everybody?' said Barbie gloomily. 'They all write a lot, but don't *do* anything.' She accepted the hot mug. 'I just want out, Sasha. I'm serious.'

'It's a big step. You've worked damned hard to get this far.'

'I realise that. But I just don't like the patients—they irritate me—especially the dirty ones, and those that smoke like chimneys and then come to have their bronchitis cured, or their obstructive airways disease, and heart attacks. I'm not cut out for the job—I know it's late to find out, but I've had enough, and I'm resigning.' She clutched the mug with both hands and sipped, while a tear dripped slowly down her pale cheek from eyes that were ringed with dark hollows.

Sasha said slowly, 'Well, it's your decision, but I'd imagine the powers-that-be would advise that you take a fortnight off sick, and then finish your six months—it's in the contract. Do you think you could manage that?'

'Not at the moment.'

Sasha felt her noble mood coming on. 'Look, just this once I'll do tonight for you, let you get your sleep. You'll probably sleep like a baby now you've got it all off your chest. Things have a way of looking less gloomy in the mornings. All of a sudden you might think you can see yourself as a consultant one day!'

Barbie didn't laugh. 'It's not funny. I'll never make it. I'm one of those who did medicine because I was bright in the sixth form—not because I wanted to help people.'

'Do you want me to do tonight or not?' Sasha stood with hands on hips. 'I've had a full day in Cas, but I'm not on my knees yet.'

'No, Sasha. Let them get the registrar.'

Sasha took the mugs to the sink and rinsed them. 'You know, the first year is the hardest. I remember lying here and thinking it was like swimming in treacle—you labour all day and all night and get nowhere. But all of a sudden it's over, and you're registered—and you start being ambitious again.'

'You're doing your Primary Fellowship, aren't you?
Going to be a famous lady surgeon?'

'Could be,' grinned Sasha. 'The exam is in January.'

'You might even work for Adam Harrington.'

Sasha smiled. 'Wouldn't mind that—he's dishy as
well as clever. It's the greying temples that do it. Why
do men look more attractive with silvery hair, while
women just look old? It's not fair.'

'Eyes off—you've got your faithful Joe!' At least
Barbie was making jokes at last. But Sasha's eyes
clouded. Joe was a problem she still had to solve.

'I'll go to the ward. You get some proper sleep, and
we'll talk again tomorrow.'

The sister on Barbie's ward was glad to see Sasha. 'I
knew Dr Green wasn't well. She had to deal with two
emergencies—didn't get to sleep till five.'

'And didn't sleep then. Who do you want me to see?'
Sasha took the cards. 'What's this? Someone given the
wrong drugs? That's serious, Sister. Anticonvulsants to
the patient who doesn't need them—do you know which
nurse it was?'

'I do, Doctor, but what good will it do to shout? The
girls these days are all the same—heads full of pop
music and boys.' Sister clicked her tongue.

Sasha allowed herself a smile. She said drily, 'I don't
think you or I were any different.'

'In my day the job came first.'

'I think it does for most of them. And look at the way
they have to walk across that dark area. How many
attacks have there been this year? Three? Four?' She
looked out of the window where the rain beat wildly and
the wind blew in the bleak trees.

Sister said, 'Three assaults and one attempted rape.'

'Not exactly one of the perks of the job.'

It was midnight when she had completed the work on
the ward. 'Just bleep me if you need me,' she said,
hoping that after last night's disturbances the ward
would be quiet. She walked along the dim corridor, the

only sound being her rubber soles whispering against the floor and the rain pattering on the dirty windows. Liverpool on a cold autumn night was not her favourite place. She pulled her coat closer around her and prepared to cross the darkened patch of ground at a run. Even the night prowler wouldn't be out in this weather, but all the same she prepared to make a run for it.

'It's Sasha Norton, isn't it?'

She swung round. Adam Harrington was approaching along the other corridor. He was wearing soft-soled shoes, too, and she hadn't heard him because of the rain. 'Hello, sir.'

'Working late? This isn't your department, is it?'

'Just popped up to help out in the ward.'

Adam's eyes widened and his dark brows lifted slightly. 'But you've done a day's work, Doctor. Want to kill yourself?'

'The houseman wasn't well. Didn't sleep last night.'

'Mmm—things don't change for housemen. It was twelve years ago when I did it. The pay has gone up a bit, but somehow nothing's been done about the hours.' He smiled at her. 'Tell your friend to keep his sense of humour.'

Sasha shrugged. 'That's easy to say——'

'From the heights of a consultant? Yes, I suppose you're right. Once we make it up that ladder, we tend to forget how ghastly it is to go without sleep because there's just no one else to take over. Well, Dr Norton, I haven't forgotten.'

The rain was still falling, a persistent, cold drizzle that soaked everything, gave the houses and trees a dead look, and wet the fallen brown leaves. Sasha began to wonder why the consultant was here at midnight. Perhaps he was happier here than going home to a lonely house. She had heard that his wife had died when they had only been married for five years. That was sad, for such a nice man. Adam Harrington, suddenly brisk, said, 'Well, my dear, perhaps I'd better walk across with you. You can't be too careful at this time of night—and that "Western Prowler" could be around.'

'Thank you very much.' She was used to going alone, but was very glad of his company. There were too many dark nooks and corners in this former workhouse, too many alleys and doorways where villains could lurk. Adam Harrington turned up his raincoat-collar and opened the door. The rain hit their faces as he took her arm and strode with her across the car park. He was just a head taller than she, and his closeness made her feel both safe and slightly exhilarated.

They reached the shelter of the brick porch, and she was sorry, because he would leave her now. 'OK?' He paused in the doorway while she took out her key.

'It's very good of you.'

'Not at all. It was like a ray of sunshine, meeting you on such a night, when all I expected was rain. Well, goodnight, Sasha.'

'Goodnight, sir.'

He shook his head. 'Don't make me feel old. My name is Adam.'

'Oh, but I shouldn't——'

'Oh, but you must!' And, with a smile and a little wave, he turned and strode off towards the dark shape of his Rover. Sasha stood, a sheet of diagonal rain almost hiding him from her as he started the car and drove out of the car park towards the deserted road. Adam . . . Could she really be so informal? He was very young for a consultant—and she wouldn't hesitate had he been a registrar. And he was nice—so very thoughtful.

'Goodnight, Adam,' she whispered to the empty car park before turning and running upstairs, the sound of his engine fading in the gusts of wind through the desolate trees. A ray of sunshine—that was a sweet thing to say. And it was how she'd felt too—seeing his handsome form appearing in the gloomy corridor. What a nice way to end a hard day. She turned her key and pushed open her front door. There was a lamp on—surely *she* hadn't left it on? Her heart thumped as she pushed open the door into the living-room. 'Joe! What are you doing here?'

He rose from the armchair, and it wasn't the Joe she used to know, but a dark-faced, threatening stranger. His voice was thick and slow. 'Where the hell have you been?'

'Working. I did the evening for Barbie Green because she's not well.' She kept her voice casual. She didn't want a fight.

'That wasn't Barbie Green you came home with!'

'Joe, don't be silly. That was Mr Harrington, and he was just seeing me across the car park because of the prowler. I only met him at the door.' The prowler. She looked at Joe, in his dark anorak and jeans, his face almost hidden by a scarf, and she felt a sudden thrill of fear. 'Joe?'

He hadn't spoken to her like this before. Was he drunk, perhaps? Yet when Joe had a couple of drinks he became pleasanter, funnier—not angry and ugly. He growled, 'You took a hell of a long time to come in, seeing you hardly know the guy.'

She felt herself blushing, not because anything had happened, but because she had enjoyed those few moments of chat more than she ought. 'We chatted for a moment.'

'Kiss you goodnight, did he?'

'Don't be a wally, Joe.' Sasha didn't know how to cope with this sudden suspicion. 'He's a senior consultant.'

'And a senior consultant is a better snogger than a mere physiotherapist?'

Sasha felt trapped. Whatever she said he jumped on like a hungry wolf. 'Don't—Joe, please don't. I'm tired, and I never meant to hurt you in any way, and I never will. I was on my way to meet you when I heard Barb crying, and I went to see what I could do.' The glow of happiness she had come in with had been replaced with a misery that matched the dreariness of

the night. 'And don't ever say a "mere physiotherapist"
like that. You've always been a true friend to me, all the
times when I needed a friend. All the time I've known
you, you've never said anything so silly.'

'I suppose I ought to say thanks for staying with me
so long.'

'Joe, please!' Tears stung her eyes. How could nice,
steady Joe alter so much? 'You'd better go. I'll see you
tomorrow.'

'That's kind of you. If you don't meet any
consultants, you mean.' He made for the door, his
shoulders hunched. That was unusual too—he was a
bodybuilder, proud of his erect stance and his broad
shoulders. He turned at the door. 'You make me very
sad sometimes.'

'I swear I never mean to. See you at the Everyman?'
She followed him to the door, wanting to forget
everything that he had said tonight. But his face was so
forbidding that she said no more than, 'Goodnight,
Joe.'

'Night.' And he slammed the door before she could
reach it. She heard his footsteps running down the
stairs, and then the outside door slammed too. That
wasn't fair. He knew the other doctors needed their
sleep, and he had never done that before. She went to
the window. The curtain was pulled back where he must
have been standing, watching as she came back home
side by side with Adam Harrington.

Surely just seeing her with another man couldn't have
triggered off this outburst? Joe just wasn't like that. She
watched him, walking as though in a hurry to get away,
his hands deep in his anorak pockets, his face half-
covered by his scarf and collar, just as a criminal would
hide his face . . . He put his head down further against
the driving rain.

Tears started as she drew the curtains against the
night. Joe wasn't like that—he'd never spoken to her
except as a good friend. He'd always been a friend—a
nice, reliable, happy-go-lucky friend . . . She shook her

head sadly. The man who strode away from here was not Joe Acourt. He might have had the same body, but the inner man—that wasn't Joe. The man who had glared at her through those blue eyes, who had showed sexual jealousy against an innocent friend—that wasn't Joe. And who else did she have, if she lost Joe?

CHAPTER TWO

THE dregs of Saturday night's casualties were still very much in evidence when Sasha went to AED the next morning, her heart and mind both strangely troubled. Two policemen were waiting to take into custody a couple of boys who had been fighting. Sasha pushed her own problems behind her and went straight to Sister Holloway. 'Need any help?'

'Am I glad to see you, Doctor. The houseman is stitching up these two villains. I don't know—kids today—they ought to have more pride.' Sister Holloway, a West Indian, sighed. Sasha knew that if more people were like Sister Holloway the world would be a better place. Sister went on, 'There's a woman with chest pains, Doctor. It doesn't sound like a heart attack, but I know it's better to be safe than sorry.'

'Get an ECG, Sister.'

'I already sent her—I knew you'd want it. They said they'll have the print-out to you in a couple of minutes.'

'Well done. Thanks.' She smiled up at the bulky Sister before turning to the woman, who sat quietly in the chair, looking tired, but not particularly ill. 'Now, are you on any tablets from your own doctor?'

The woman seemed to be happy when explaining about herself. 'For me blood pressure, yes. And these . . .' She struggled to produce a bottle of tablets from her damp coat pocket. 'These are for me pain.'

Sasha looked at the label. 'These are for your stomach, Mrs—' she checked the name on the card—'Mrs Delaney. Have you an ulcer?'

'No, Doctor—I had an X-ray of me stomach.'

No ulcer. Sasha pondered. 'Have you been in the Western before?'

'Two year ago—for me blood pressure.'

Sister Holloway read Sasha's look. 'I'll check if her notes are here.'

The long strip of ECG print-out was handed to Sasha then. She checked carefully. The ST segment was depressed, and the T waves were definitely inverted. Sasha wasted no time in getting to the phone. 'Coronary unit, please.' She waited, tapping her fingers. 'Chris? Another CI, I'm afraid. Can I send her straight up? Lady of fifty-five, been here about four hours, poor soul. Not in a lot of pain, but definite changes in the ECG.'

'I'm sorry, Sasha—I'm not discharging anyone till tomorrow. Absolutely no beds. Can't you send her to a medical ward?'

'Can't one of your less ill patients go to a medical ward?'

'I'll check, just for you. Oh, send her up. She'll have to stay in the middle of the ward for a while, but we can get her on a monitor.'

'Thanks, Chris.'

'Don't mention it—I've done my stint down there, I know what it's like. Have they mended that broken door?'

'Yes, they have, but no one's been to mop the floor. We might as well see patients in the car park, for all the hygiene there is in here.'

Chris Low laughed. 'Not quite that bad. Cheer up—not long now till you join the privileged classes upstairs.'

'I can hardly wait.'

She went back to work. The chat with Chris had lightened her mood slightly, but all the time at the back of her mind lurked her worries about Joe. It wasn't like him to be jealous of anyone. Last night he had shown a side of himself she'd never known existed. Yet how could she have known him for four years without noticing this trait in his character?

One of the policemen tapped at the door. 'Doctor,

will my man be long? I don't want him to slip out by another door. It's taken me four months to get a charge that'll stick, and I don't want to lose him now.'

'Don't worry. He's still in the cubicle with my colleague.'

'Thanks.' The policeman winked. 'Doctors are getting younger—and definitely prettier.' Sasha smiled, accepting the compliment happily.

Sister Holloway was back with Mrs Delaney's notes. Sasha checked them quickly. Yes, the patient had been in the Western with hypertension and a query hiatus hernia. That was why she was carrying Tagamet, even though her barium meal showed up no ulcer. Sasha scanned the previous history. Yes, there was a note that she had complained of pains in her chest, possibly due to angina pectoris. Good job Mrs Delaney had had the sense to ring her sister and get herself brought in today. With treatment she should recover from her heart attack. She looked an anxious woman—perhaps she needed advice about diet. Sasha smiled to herself—so often patients resented being told to change their life-style. Doctors were here to heal, not to preach!

Sister shouted in her booming voice, 'Telephone for you, Doctor.'

Sasha went to the phone. It was Joe, and he sounded much more like his old self. 'I had to ring, Sasha. No hard feelings?'

'I can't pretend I wasn't hurt, Joe. I have so much to think about, and worrying over you doesn't make my job any easier.'

'I don't know what came over me—a sort of tension inside—and I did feel annoyed that Harrington might take advantage of you.'

'That's rot—he's a gentleman, Joe Acourt.'

'Gentlemen, as you call them, are as bad as anyone else when they fancy someone—sometimes worse. Just you see.'

'Joe, I'm too busy to discuss this now. Call me tonight, OK?' She went back to work, her heart thumping. What on earth made easygoing Joe suddenly make a big fuss about nothing? Was he under some sort of stress at work that she didn't know about? She owed him the benefit of the doubt. They could talk tonight. Perhaps . . .

There was a sudden shout—'Look out, he's getting away!' There were running feet and scrambled cries, and the constable whipped round with a speed she wouldn't have thought possible for a man of his bulk, in full cry after the runaway youth. There was a crash as a trolley of instruments was knocked over. There wasn't much hope of the boy getting away, but he had the careless attitude of someone for whom nothing really mattered anyway—even a brief chase relieved the boredom and ignorance of his young life. He was brought to the ground with a rugby tackle, and screamed as he hit his already stitched face on the wall. He gave up tamely, walking firmly held by the policeman, an expression of blank indifference in his eyes.

Sasha turned to go back to her work, only to find the slim, smart figure of Adam Harrington looking for her. With a friendly gesture he called her over. 'If you'd like to come up and see your patient . . . He is very grateful to you for your excellent treatment, it seems, and he'd like to thank you. He will be in theatre this morning, having his femur pinned, but feel free to pop up—he'll be nursed in my department.'

Sasha felt guilty—and angry with Joe for making her feel guilty when she was only discussing a patient with a colleague. 'Thank you. I will.'

Adam smiled. 'Fine. Ring me when you're coming, and we'll take a look at him together.' He went towards the lift. Sasha knew her cheeks had gone pink. The staff in the Western were overworked and harassed. Any sign of gossip made a welcome change—and a single, attractive consultant was always fair game. Sasha herself was always being teased for having no steady boyfriend—Joe was always around, but no one took it seriously.

Philip Mortimer called her over. 'Take a look at this, Sasha.' She thought he had an interesting case for her to see, but he was standing in the cubicle, pointing at a single, diminutive domestic, complete with electric cleaner. 'What a vision of loveliness! Even though she's four hours late.'

The little woman heard that. 'It's orright, queen—Wonder Woman is 'ere. We're short-staffed, luv, but I'll soon 'ave yer sorted out.'

'Thanks very much.' Sasha's thanks were heartfelt. The good-natured woman was soon working away at the filthy floor, and, as the number of patients dwindled, the department at last started to regain its original colour scheme. The voluntary tea-lady came and opened up her stall, and Sasha went back to the office with a plastic cup of what was supposed to be coffee.

Later she went to the doctors' common-room. She saw Adam in a corner chatting with the others from his department. She went across to sit by Barbie Green, who was gazing into space, her white coat crumpled on her lap. 'Better, Barb?'

'Less tired. But I still can't make myself like the work any more. I just don't want to be a doctor.'

Sasha sat down by her. 'You could do desk work—or be a school MO. They are nine-to-five jobs. And not much customer hassle.'

'I can't plan anything just now—not in the middle of a bad case of reactive depression.'

Sasha tried to be hearty. 'Never mind—you're not the first, and you won't be the last. Think of it as par for the course. And Christmas is coming—that should be fun. I enjoy Christmas on the wards.'

Barbara shook her head. 'When the tinsel comes off it will be ten times worse. But thanks for trying, Sasha. I'll go and have a word with Dr Slade, I think. Maybe he can give me some anti-depressants.'

Sasha said, 'I've had a brainwave! Why don't I cook you a delicious meal—full of vitamins and healthy things? I'll ask Joe—he needs cheering up, too. How about it? Saturday night?'

'Sounds nice.' But Barbie's lacklustre eyes denied her words. 'The trouble is, when anyone's nice to me, I start crying.' Her eyes filled. 'Don't look like that, Sasha. I'm not suicidal yet.'

'I didn't mean . . .' But Sasha knew that depressives just might turn into overdoses. 'Give me a buzz if you need anyone to make inane conversation, OK?' She patted Barbie's shoulder and went to the door.

'Hello, Sasha.' It was Adam, who had separated himself from his friends. 'You're coming up later to see old Jonesy?'

'Yes, of course.'

'I—hear there's a staff party on Saturday. Do you usually go?'

'Usually.' What was he leading up to? 'But I'm busy this week.'

'I see.' He nodded, and walked away rather fast. Sasha looked after him, and wondered why she wanted to run after him. Harrington was nothing to Sasha Norton—yet within the last twenty-four hours something had happened to make her terribly aware of him. It must be Joe—yes, that was it—Joe's insane jealousy last night had turned a normal relationship between two colleagues into an illicit affair almost. She was glad she had sorted that out. She walked back to Casualty slowly, still thinking hard.

There was a man with an indirect inguinal hernia lying on the couch when she got back. He was young, with a typical light-hearted approach to his problem. ''Sorright, queen, prod it about if yer want. I 'ave ter purrit back meself every evening before I go out ter the pub.'

She smiled as she examined him carefully. 'You're going to need surgery, Mr Wright, one of these days. The muscle is very lax indeed, and it will need tightening up and stitching. I'll just call one of the surgeons to take a look at you.'

'Aw, can't you do it, luv? You've got nice gentle 'ands.'

She looked up into his cheerful face and smiled again. 'I'm not a surgeon—yet.'

''Ow long will it take for you ter be one?'

'Three or four years at the earliest.'

'OK, that'll do. Give me a call in three years.' And he pretended to get up to go home.

'Sit down, Mr Wright, while I get you a proper surgeon.'

The young registrar prodded the lump and made a few mumbling noises. 'This must be uncomfortable, Mr Wright. I'm afraid there is quite a queue for this type of surgery, but I'll put your name on the list.'

The man looked up at him quizzically. 'I bet if I said I'd go private, you'd do me termorrer.'

'No, I wouldn't—I don't do private work.'

'Burr I thought all you doctors——'

'Well, you thought wrong.' The registrar gave him a final pat before leaving the cubicle and saying to Sasha quietly, 'Do you get much abuse?'

'Funnily enough, not a lot.'

He smiled. 'Maybe it helps being a beautiful woman?'

'Sexist,' she said to his retreating back. 'But thanks.'

By the end of the day she was feeling extremely tired, as the night she had done for Barbara caught up with her. But, although her eyes were closing and she hardly could be bothered to comb her hair, she knew she had to go up to Adam's ward to see 'old Jonesy'. She realised she had been looking forward to it all day, and trying to push away the idea that she was going up in the hope of chatting to Adam Harrington again.

He was in his room, busy with some papers. 'I'll be with you in a moment, Doctor,' he said shortly. She felt very much put in her place, very much the junior doctor. What had made her think he would welcome her any other way? They had only made each other's acquaintance last night. She waited quietly in the corridor outside his room, feeling slightly uncomfortable, as though her visit was a nuisance to a busy man.

Pat Moore, Harrington's senior registrar, came along just then. 'Hello, Dr—Norton, isn't it? Can I help you at all?'

'I only came up to see Mr Jones. How is he?'

'Our neck of femur patient? He's OK—conscious, but not all that conscious, if you see what I mean. Come along, I'll show you where he is.'

'Er—Mr Harrington—told to me to wait.'

'Oh, Adam will come along later.' Pat breezed along the corridor, explaining about the operation and what treatment they were giving Jonesy now. 'He should be able to go home within a fortnight. Trouble is, he lives alone.' They entered the ward, and Pat led her to an alcove of four beds. The old man lay on his back, still connected to a drip, which Pat took down before gently shaking him. 'Mr Jones, you wanted to see Dr Norton.'

The old man gave a crooked smile as he recognised Sasha, and tried to hold out his right hand. But, obviously, that was the side affected by the stroke, and Sasha quickly took his other hand and allowed him to shake hers warmly. 'You were so kind. Even in the middle of all that noise, with people all over the place.' His voice was slightly affected, but she could easily hear the appreciation in it. 'I was a piece of meat on a slab to most people. But you came along, and called me by my name, and made me feel that I was being looked after in spite of the chaos. Up till then I had been terrified.'

'I didn't realise that.' She hadn't given him any special treatment. 'Still, you feel fine now?'

'Much better. Mr Harrington is kind too, but he's a busy man.'

'Not all that busy, Mr Jones!' Adam was suddenly on the opposite side of the bed.

He grinned up with one side of his mouth. 'Call me Jonesy, sir—I used to be a schoolmaster, and the boys always called me that—I take it as a sign of affection.'

Adam said gently, 'I'm sure it was, I'm sure it was.' And, after a few more encouraging remarks, Sasha took her leave of him, feeling warm and grateful for his thanks. As they walked along the corridor, Adam said, 'Why didn't you wait for me?'

Pat Moore said, 'Oops! My fault. I thought I'd save you a little trouble.'

Adam laughed. 'I wouldn't call Dr Norton trouble if I were you, Pat.'

'But you have a lot to do, Mr Harrington—I can see I'm interrupting you,' said Sasha quickly.

Pat said tactfully, 'I've just remembered—I must see that child we operated on yesterday. I promised to say goodnight to him.' And with a spurt he covered the distance they had just travelled along the corridor in two or three seconds. Sasha felt herself reddening. It was as though the senior registrar had recognised that his two companions had more to say to each other. Sasha was suddenly scared at the implication of his sudden departure—it meant that he understood that his chief wanted some time alone with the casualty SHO. And, as that SHO, she saw herself being the centre of all the latest gossip about poor Adam, which she never wanted to happen.

'Well, I'll be off, too.' Tongue-tied, she could think of nothing to say, nothing that could hold her in his company any longer, even though he didn't appear to want to get back to any work. 'Goodnight, sir—I mean, Adam.'

He smiled, and regarded her with his handsome grey eyes. 'That's better. 'Night, Sasha. Thanks for coming up.' And as she went down in the lift she thought again how charming and approachable he was. Only when she walked away from the lift did she overhear the two nurses who had come down with her discussing her.

'Is Dr Norton the latest, then?'

'Looks like it. I don't fancy her chances—she's too quiet. But I saw the way she stared up at him—like a pet dog. Some hopes, eh? She'll end up another Sister

Pearce.'

'How long do you give them?'

Sasha had walked out of earshot and did not hear the reply. This sort of gossip was only to be expected. She had been in the Department of Neuro-surgery for about twenty-minutes, and already the grapevine was predicting heartbreak for Dr Norton. She smiled quietly to herself—the nurses were wrong about one thing. She didn't gaze at Adam like an adoring pet dog. She had only visited the department because old Jonesy wanted to thank her. Therefore, she would have to disappoint the nurses by not going floppy over their precious Mr Harrington. She drew her shoulders back and made her way to the mess. There was just one thing—who was Sister Pearce, and how did she end up? The thought stayed with her for at least another five minutes, before the thought of food superseded it.

When Joe Acourt presented himself at Sasha's flat the following Saturday evening, Sasha looked at him keenly for any signs of his dreadful mood of their last meeting. But he seemed almost his usual self, with a smile on his face and a bottle of wine in his hand. 'Hello, love. Something smells good. Your pal here yet?' He went in and pulled off his anorak before giving her a kiss on the cheek. 'It's cold out. Wouldn't be surprised if we had a touch of frost.'

She unwrapped the bottle. 'This is lovely, Joe. Could you open it and give me an egg-cupful to put in the sauce? Barbie isn't here—I went down earlier, but she isn't in yet. I do hope she hasn't forgotten. I know she isn't on duty.'

Joe stood in the tiny kitchen and helped with the wine and setting the table. Barbara still hadn't arrived, and Sasha finally said, 'Joe, we'd better go and find her. Be a dear and ring her bell again, while I just put something a bit more hostessy on.' She went to the bedroom and found a slim black dress that had long sleeves, to protect her against the chill of the night. Joe came back without Barbara Green.

'There's a dance on in the mess—I heard the din. You don't think she went with someone else?'

'We can only go and see.' Sasha put the dishes in the oven to keep warm. 'If I were depressed I wouldn't go to a dance, but you never know. Let's go—I'm not having my cordon bleu chicken wasted.' They ran across to the main building and into the warm. In the mess a Nigerian surgeon was in charge of a case of brown ale, and a large Welsh charge nurse was distributing cocktails under a festoon of tinsel. The music was very loud, as usual, and the flashing lights alternated with patches of extreme dimness. Sasha and Joe accepted a drink as they prowled round trying to find their friend among embracing couples and gyrating dancers.

'Sasha, I thought you weren't coming tonight.' She knew who it was before she turned and saw Adam Harrington in dark trousers and a loose sweater, dancing with one of his theatre sisters.

Against the music, she shouted, 'Looking for Barbie. She was supposed to come to my place.' Adam nodded and was swallowed up by other dancers. Sasha watched his dark head, the silver hidden by the strobe lights, and his face looking incredibly young as he moved with unexpected abandon that made it clear that their senior consultant had a very nice figure.

Joe said in her ear, 'Are we looking for Barb, or admiring Harrington's bum?'

She turned away, colouring and glad of the camouflage of the lights. Joe's tone hinted at the unpleasant things he had said about Adam last time, and she didn't want the evening spoiled. 'Let's go. She clearly isn't here.' She shouldered her way through the crowd.

Adam was in the corridor. 'Have you found your friend?'

'No, she isn't at the party.' Sasha drew Joe forward. 'You know Joe Acourt, Adam?'

He held out his hand. 'Everyone knows Joe,' he said

with a grin. 'You did a world of good for my shoulder when I strained it playing squash. How are you?'

'OK.' Joe's tone gave nothing away.

Adam said, 'This girl—is it the one you did a locum for last weekend?'

They confirmed it. 'I promised her a meal tonight, but she hasn't turned up, and there are no lights in her flat.'

Adam's face showed concern. 'I think we ought to go back to her flat. Just in case. You said she was feeling the strains of housemanship. We had a sister—she was depressed too, and they found her—well, let's not talk about it—let's go and make sure she isn't at home before we get frightened.'

He led the way across the dark quadrangle, with only a few cars parked there now. He said, 'And there's the "Western Prowler" to worry about, too.' He broke into a run.

They stood together outside Barbie's closed and dark flat. Sasha rang and rang. 'Surely she wouldn't be so daft as to take an overdose!' She banged again, and then called shrilly through the letter-box, 'Hey, Barbie, grub's up!' She stood erect and faced the two men. They stood holding their breath, listening, worried.

Then they all let out their breath with relief as a shuffling sound on the other side of the door heralded the arrival of a very sleepy houseman in dressing-gown and slippers, her red-gold hair in lank locks round a face pink with sleep. She stared, her blue eyes opening wide at the reception that greeted her. 'I say, I'm most terribly sorry. I took two Mogadon. Is it too late?'

Sasha laughed with relief. 'Go and put your head under a tap, and join us in ten minutes. The wine is open.' She saw that Adam was preparing to leave them, and said impulsively, 'Would you like to come too, Adam? Chicken à la Norton?'

'That's very decent of you—my mouth has been watering at the smell since we came in. You sure it's all right?'

Sasha assured him that it was, and she was greatly relieved when Joe said, 'Sure. Come along and make the table symmetrical. She's cooked enough veg for an army.'

'It's good for you!' Laughing, Sasha led the way up to her own flat.

Joe poured wine for them. 'I've never had a meal with a brain surgeon before,' he confided, with a touch of his old cheerful openness that had first attracted the quiet, shy Sasha.

Adam lifted his glass to him. 'They do other things, you know, Joe, like play squash, and wash socks, and eat curry and watch football——'

'You watch Liverpool?' Joe's eyes lit up.

'Of course. Who else?'

Joe sat beside him on the sofa. 'How do you think they're doing this season? Do you think they ought to be higher in the league by this month?' And Sasha went back to the kitchen, relieved and delighted that there weren't going to be any awkward pauses in the conversation at table.

She heard Adam reply, 'In my opinion they ought . . .' and she inspected her roast potatoes with a smile on her lips. How sweet of Adam to be concerned about Barbie. She arrived in a loose cheesecloth dress, her hair brushed and her eyes a lot brighter then they had been at first. The two girls served the food, Barbie making little squeaks of excitement as she kept producing her favourites from the oven.

'Ooh, broccoli—I love that! Cauliflower in onion sauce. However did you get the potatoes so golden?'

'Because you were asleep. I hope they're not too hard!'

Over the meal, Adam prodded Barbie about her state of mind. Sasha could tell that his questions were aimed at finding out how depressed she was. The atmosphere was friendly and warm, so that Barbie found herself answering his questions frankly. Adam explained why he had taken an interest. 'We had this girl in our department—three or four years ago, now. She hid all her feelings, and then—well—it was almost too late.'

'I won't do anything stupid, but it's so nice of you all to take trouble for me like this.' Barbie was quite overwhelmed by the evening, and tears started in her eyes. 'I promise not to take an overdose. Don't forget—I've seen how horrid it is when you have to use a stomach pump!' She stood up to clear the table with Sasha. In a moment, Adam was at the sink, running hot water and squeezing liquid in. 'No, don't stop me—I'm good at this. It will be done by the time you've made coffee.' And, as they all joined in to help, Adam went on, 'Barbara, when are you due for a holiday?'

'Christmas, I suppose.'

'Sasha?'

'Me, too.'

Adam finished scouring the last pan. 'I have a small place in the Ionian.' The statement was greeted by the other three with utter stillness, Joe stopping with the coffee-jug half-way to a cup, and Barbie with a pile of plates ready to put into the cupboard. As Sasha echoed his last word, Adam went on, 'I'm not going out this winter. Zaramos is a place where anyone can unwind, I promise you. It's yours for a fortnight, if you want it.' He emptied the water and turned round, smiling. 'Well?'

'Do you really mean it?'

'Sure. It's just what you need. Two weeks of sun. Don't thank me, because I'm always glad if someone goes out and looks after it for me. And the cat will be pleased to have company.'

When they had overcome their shock, the questions came from all sides as they sat at the kitchen table to drink their coffee. 'Boat? I haven't one of my own, but there's a friend of mine who will take you out any time.' He explained more fully. 'Actually, he's the local GP on the island, and we met in London when we were both doing exams. It's more of a cottage than a villa—but the beach is only yards away, so it's ideal for relaxing and forgetting about bad weather and crowded wards.'

Barbara said dreamily, 'I can't believe that this is happening. I can't imagine anything nicer anyone could have done for me. You're very clever at making people feel better, Adam—and very kind, too.'

He smiled, seemingly pleased at her reaction. 'I'm only too glad to have colleagues visit—it keeps the vandals away, and pleases the cat.'

Sasha watched him, already his fan, but now even more grateful to him. From being a distant, revered figure, Adam Harrington had very rapidly become almost a friend. She knew that in hospital life one often became close with people one worked with—only to leave and never see them again. But, at the back of her mind, she hoped that wouldn't happen here. The evening had been one of the best she could remember.

Adam said, 'I must tell you, Sasha, that I've enjoyed this evening more than any I can remember for a long time.' And Sasha blushed again as his words so closely echoed her thoughts.

Barbara said, 'Hear, hear to that—but my Mogadon is catching up with me again.'

'You mean we're not going on to the mess party?' teased Joe.

'Not me, Joe. After all that super food? Goodnight, everyone, and thank you all for being so nice to me.' Barbie stood up and kissed Sasha. 'You're a wonderful cook—I'm truly grateful.' She turned to Joe. 'You're such good company, Joe—you'd make anyone feel better.' She turned to Adam last. 'I think the picture of that villa will swim before my eyes for the next two months. Thank you, sir, so very much.' And as he raised his hand she said, 'Adam, I mean. I can't tell you how much better I feel since I walked into this flat a couple of hours ago.'

Adam said, 'I'll see you down, Barbie. I must be off, too.' And, within minutes, all that was left of their guests were four coffee-cups and a plate of grape seeds.

Sasha yawned. 'Gosh, that went so well!'

The night was still outside. Joe stood up, and the look had gone from his eyes. In its place was coldness, even threat. He said quietly, 'That man wants to sleep with you.'

'Joe!'

'Don't come all that stuff with me. I saw the way he looked at you—at your body. I warn you—it won't be long before he starts.'

'Joe, he's a nice man, that's all. You liked him too. You were talking away like mad.'

'Fair enough—but I still felt mad at the way he was eyeing you all the time. Then offering you a holiday—it was like buying you! It's hideous to me, Sasha, hideous!'

Sasha felt again that the man with her wasn't Joe Acourt, but a total and frightening stranger. There was nothing she could say that could take that blank, staring look from his once dear familiar face——

'Joe, you were never petty-minded——'

'Just tell me the truth,' he stormed. 'Just tell me—if you were here with Harrington alone—you would have gone to bed with him, wouldn't you?'

'What sort of man do you think he is, for goodness' sake?'

Joe said quietly, between his teeth, 'A man, of course. Just a man.' And he suddenly pulled her to her feet, held her tightly against him, and covered her face and lips with hard, unfeeling kisses. This wasn't Joe—never and she was scared, suddenly very scared. He said, his voice hoarse in her ear, 'Come on, girl—I saw the way you looked at Harrington. I'm not bloody blind, Sasha. Give some of that to me, my friend—it's about time, surely? Come on, Sasha, come on!' His voice rose suddenly as he gripped her chin and forced her mouth open to receive his kisses.

When she managed to wrench her head away, she gasped, 'I don't want to hate you, Joe, so please leave me alone. I feel sick, Joe—I have to go and lie down.

Please, Joe, please . . .'

And, just as suddenly as he had taken her in his arms, his arms fell to his sides, and he said, his voice almost a whisper, 'Sometimes I feel wretched, Sasha. Will I ever be worthy of you?'

She could only stare, wondering and scared at the change in him. 'Joe—go and see Dr Slade—please? Tell him all this. You might be under some stress at work—need something to calm you down——'

He crashed his fist on the table, making the coffee-cups rattle in the saucers. 'I'm not a bloody loony, woman. If I need tablets, I'll take tablets. All I want now is for you to be faithful to me, not be so shameless in front of Barbie. She must think you're the next thing to a prostitute, the way you fussed over that bloody consultant.'

She summoned courage, took a deep breath. 'Get out now, Joe. I don't want to talk with you any longer. I'm not well, and I must get some sleep.' Something in her voice got through to him then. He went to the front door and opened it, standing for a moment, then turning to look at her. Sasha stayed where she was, her head high, her cheeks burning with suppressed anger and fear. Joe closed the door behind him, his head hanging low as he turned and left her.

She waited. She knew he hadn't gone downstairs. She put off the lights and went to the bedroom, but she knew she couldn't sleep until she had seen him leave the building. She went stealthily to the front window. The lighted clock in the hospital tower showed half-past twelve. She waited, just looking at the bleak car park, at the few leaves left on the two thin sycamores, waving woefully in the breeze. The clock showed one o'clock before Joe's sturdy figure emerged from the doctors' residence and crossed the car park to the exit. She sighed with relief as she bolted the front door, and then changed into her nightshirt.

She took one last look through the living-room window before turning in. Then she gasped. Joe was still there, his anorak collar up round his face, leaning against one of the sycamores, staring into space. She began to think again of the prowler—how many nurses had been attacked—Joe was strong, she knew—and just now he was behaving abnormally. It had just never entered her head that he could do anything dreadful. Now her heart beat fast as she scrambled into bed and pulled the duvet right over her head. She was shivering.

The phone rang. She got up and took it with a trembling hand. 'Yes?'

'You OK?'

She tried to stop her voice shaking. 'Yes, thank you, Joe.'

'You didn't go to the party, then?'

'Is that why——?' She stopped herself. 'I told you—I feel ill.'

'I'm sorry, kid—get some sleep.'

She lay for a long time, alert and worried. Joe had thought she would go to the party, perhaps in the hope of seeing Adam. Why should he be so perturbed about Adam Harrington? Did he see more than she did?

CHAPTER THREE

IT WAS lucky for Sasha that she was studying for her Primary Fellowship exam. Losing herself in her books was the ideal solution to the strained atmosphere between her and Joe Acourt. When they did meet in the mess or in the hospital, they spoke almost as strangers. She realised that his outspoken references to Adam Harrington had been partly due to the wine having loosened his tongue. All the same, when she met Adam in the corridors or the common-room, she felt embarrassed by Joe's accusations. Adam was politeness itself when they chatted—but Sasha knew that she was finding him increasingly attractive, and blaming Joe for putting the ideas into her head. By his wild accusations, Joe had almost made his own suspicions come true. Poor Sasha made every effort to put it all behind her, studying hard almost every night she was free, and making it clear to Joe that she no longer had the time to go out in the evenings.

All the same, as she ploughed her way through Anatomy again, and pored over histology slides, she longed for the days when she could just ring Joe to pop in for a coffee. His cheerful attitude used to relax her, and his Liverpudlian knack of making a joke out of everything was a superb antidote to her own over-conscientious nature. It was like losing a friend—Joe was still around, yet not the Joe she used to know.

Barbie had improved tremendously, partly buoyed up by the promise of that holiday in the sun. She still maintained that she wasn't cut out to be a doctor, but her complaints were muted, and when the two girls met their talk was all about what clothes they would need for their Greek island, and whether it would be warm enough to swim on Christmas Day. 'Adam hasn't changed his mind yet?' Barbie would say hopefully. 'I've just spent nearly fifty pounds on a cotton suit.'

'I'm sure it's on. Adam doesn't say things he doesn't mean.'

'I do hope so. When did you last talk?'

'A while ago.' Sasha wondered if possibly Adam might be regretting his easy familiarity with his juniors. The last time she had been up to his department, he had been hosting a group of visiting professors and consultants who were listening intently to Adam expounding his latest techniques and research. The conversation was intense and serious, and she found herself on the fringe of the group, full of admiration for his fluent method of expression, and wondering if she would ever aspire to such a height of intellectual understanding of her work.

Adam was saying, 'One does need a good team of plastic surgeons to work with. You see, any reconstruction necessary can be done at the same operation, instead of putting the patient through two caraniotomies."

'But I say—in this climate? When we're all being told to cut our budgets? Surely no one can command such manpower these days?'

Adam shook his head. 'I do agree. It's not always possible, and surgery these days has to be about being practical. My argument is that one operation is cheaper than two. And the results are excellent. I've had a woman back at work in three months after total reconstruction of the frontal sinus.'

'Have you done any recently, Mr Harrington?'

'I have a couple in the ward now—we'll go along and see them.' He led the way out of his office, and noticed Sasha on the way. He paused and smiled as he caught sight of her. 'You wanted to see me, Dr Norton?'

'It can wait.' She backed away, blushing as the visiting dignitaries looked at her with varying degrees of curiosity and admiration.

Adam beckoned her. 'Join us, if you've the time. You intend to do surgery. Let me show you my patients. It all helps, you know.' And one or two of the others agreed that young surgeons ought to see as many different types of patient as they could. Sasha found herself forming part of the admiring retinue. But she found her attention wandering as she walked behind him, remembering how his elegant form had looked so young and attractive at the party, in those dark, slim-fitting trousers and the casual sweater. She looked sideways at the other surgeons, and hoped that none was a mind-reader. How was it that with every other doctor in the hospital she thought of them only as doctors, but with Adam she was immediately conscious that she was a woman speaking to a magnetic man, and unable to forget his attraction? It was all Joe's fault, for planting the idea in her head. Yet, if Joe had never voiced his suspicions, would she have walked behind this impeccable three-piece suit imagining herself listening to the gentle, cultured voice speaking words of love? As she left the room later she was glad it had not been a lecture where she had to answer questions, because she had heard not one word he'd spoken about the patients, but only listened to the cadence of his beautiful voice.

That evening she was just getting ready to go off duty, chatting to Sister Holloway about the two admissions before she left. Sister looked over her shoulder and said in her musical voice, 'Good evening, Mr Harrington. What can we do for you, sir?'

Sasha put down her used syringes, composed herself and turned round. 'Hello,' she said brightly.

Adam was casual, breezy. 'You wanted me, I think?'

She nodded. 'But you shouldn't have taken the trouble to come down. It was only about the villa.'

'Not at all—I was passing anyway. Of course—I should have contacted you with the details, so that you can book your tickets. Have you decided on dates? Because I can drop Andreas a line and tell him to expect you.'

She pushed her hair back from her eyes, feeling acutely the contrast between his well-groomed look and her end-of-the-day scruffiness. 'Well, yes, I think so. Barbara is——'

He interrupted her, saying very gently, 'Don't put your hair back. It's prettier round your face.' Sasha looked round for Sister Holloway, but that lady had tactfully made herself scarce. Adam went on, 'We could have a working dinner tonight, if you're free, and I could tell you more about Zaramos.'

His tone, suddenly warm and intimate, caused her heart to thump violently against her ribs as she recalled some of Joe's insinuations. She cleared her throat before replying. 'I'm not sure if Barbie——'

'You can tell her later.' So it was to be a twosome. She was glad, yet apprehensive. Was Joe right? 'I'll pick you up at seven.'

'Thanks.' Gosh, it was six now, and she would need to have a bath and wash her hair—that hair that he had said was pretty round her face . . . And what did one wear to have dinner with a senior consultant?

After running across to her flat in a wild surge of excitement, she flung all the clothes she had on the bed, and wished she had been more style conscious. She dried her hair, fluffing it round her face as he had said with a look that showed he found her attractive. Oh, dear—suppose he . . .? Just then the phone rang.

It was Joe. 'Can I come over tonight?'

That was all she needed. Dared she lie? She had never lied to Joe, but this Joe was different from the one who had first befriended a simple, nervous houseman. 'Can we make it tomorrow, Joe? I'm terribly busy right now.' That was true, but a lie as well, because it sounded as though she were busy with books, not dressing up for another man. She felt wretched at having to do it. 'Look forward to tomorrow, usual time?'

'I needed——' Joe's voice sounded raw, but then it

changed and he said, 'I know you have work to do. I'm sorry.' He rang off abruptly, and she suddenly had a glimpse in her mind's eye of that lonely figure leaning up against a tree in the cold, staring up at her window. Poor Joe—maybe he did need her. Maybe tonight he had been going to confess what was on his mind—and she had failed him. Yet tonight she knew that nothing would stop her having dinner with Adam Harrington.

The doorbell rang, and she flew to open it. 'Oh, come in—for a moment—I was just . . .'

Adam was wearing a casual jacket and trousers, and his shirt and tie were casual, too, not the strictly tailored things he wore at work. He said gently, 'No hurry, Sasha. We're not on duty now, remember.' His eyes crinkled at the corners when he smiled, and she gazed at him with rapt and complete devotion. He said, 'I'll just wait in the living-room.'

'I won't be long.' She tried not to run to the bedroom, where she emptied her old handbag on to the bed, scooped up the contents and stuffed them in the other, smarter bag. She was back within moments, her cheeks flushed with exertion.

He had been looking out of the window. Now he turned, and their eyes met. Within a moment he was holding her in his arms, and leaning his cheek against hers. 'Sasha, Sasha, you're so sweet, my dear. It's only me you're going out with, not the Queen of England.'

Against his chest, which smelt clean and warm and male, she said, 'That's the trouble.'

'You're very sweet,' he said again, and he bent and kissed her lips. Fireworks went off all around her, blinding her, deafening her. It was as though she had never been kissed before, and this kiss was worth the wait, as it lengthened and grew stronger. His grip tightened around her, so that their bodies were pressed close, the full length of them. After an unknowable time, he drew away. She looked up, seeing in his eyes something deep, misty and mysterious. He said, his voice very low, 'We'd better go, I think.'

'Yes.' She opened her bag to check for the key, and, because she had to scrabble for it, the atmosphere lightened between them, and they were laughing as they went downstairs, past Barbie's flat to the ground floor. It was a gloomy, sad autumn night, with the last of the brown shrivelled leaves clinging to the dismal trees in a sort of pathetic defiance. The dark blue Rover looked out of place in these dingy surroundings. As they got in, she told him so.

'Why should it? This is where I work.'

'Do you like Liverpool?'

'It's a fine city. I've no intention of going anywhere else.'

For some reason that pleased Sasha. 'Where are we going?'

'We'll have a drink at the Albert Dock, then decide. Where do you usually eat?'

'When we were students, the Wimpy Bar. Since I've been working, we don't eat out much.'

They were driving through Toxteth, where the mean terraces had been replaced by modern maisonettes, trees and green lawns. Many fine Georgian blocks had been renovated and improved, and those that didn't belong to the university were lived in by West Indians and Nigerians. Adam said, 'This Joe—your steady?'

She wondered just how to describe Joe. 'He was always one of the crowd,' she said cautiously. 'He was extrovert—just what I needed.'

'Lucky chap.'

Sasha made no response, and Adam asked no more questions as he drove along Wapping towards the gracious pink blocks, illuminated at night like some Venetian painting, reflected in the still waters of the rejuvenated docks. They parked close to the pavilions and walked together across the newly set flags. Sasha was still remembering his kiss, and wondering if that first kiss was to be followed by more.

They went downstairs to the vaulted-brick basement of the Albert Dock, where once the great bales of cotton, barrels of rum from the Indies, and molasses were stored, in the days when the city had been a proud and thriving port. Adam ordered white wine. 'I know very little about you, Sasha.'

She smiled as she explained, 'I'm so busy that there's nothing to tell. Surely you remember having no time for hobbies? Working so hard that any time off is spent sleeping or studying?'

'I do. And, if you'll allow me, I'll collect the tickets for you, as I shall be passing the travel agent's. You are looking forward to Zaramos?'

'So very much. I just can't tell you——'

'Joe doesn't mind you going?'

Sasha said quietly, 'Joe is a mystery to me, Adam. For the first three years after I met him, he was one of the jolliest boys in the gang.'

Adam agreed. 'When I went down for physio to my shoulder he was very cheerful—always making jokes and getting on famously with his staff. He seemed subdued when I came to your place for a meal. Has he changed?'

'Totally.' She paused, but there seemed no harm in confiding in Adam. 'That night after you left—he waited outside in the cold to make sure I didn't follow you to the party.'

'That could be plain old jealousy,' smiled Adam. 'Did you give him any reason to think you would follow me?'

She shook her head. 'Not a bit. I was tired.'

Adam seemed amused. 'That is bad for my self-esteem, but interesting in view of the case history. Personality changes are always symptoms, Sasha.'

'You think there's something very wrong?'

'Could be. Any other symptoms—sleeplessness, irritability?'

She had to go on, having told him so much. 'He seems very fixated about—sex. Sees it in others.' Adam nodded, apparently understanding perfectly. She went on, 'These attacks on nurses—it only occurred to me the other night—I hate to think it could be Joe, but he just isn't the Joe I've always known.'

Adam let out a soundless whistle. 'Hormonal imbalance—some sort of endocrine disorder can make men act out of character.' He reached over and loosened Sasha's fingers, which were gripping the edge of the table in her worry and pity. 'Try not to worry, my dear. The best thing to do would be to ask him straight out if he thinks he should see Slade.'

'I did mention it. I'll try again.' She looked across at him. 'I'm grateful for being able to talk to you about it.'

'I'm no ogre.'

She managed a smile. 'To juniors, aren't all consultants ogres?'

'When you think that, remember I was a junior ten years ago, and I reckon I haven't forgotten what it was like. I still have my sense of humour, too. You need that in our game.'

They laughed together and, as their eyes met, she remembered the kiss again, and looked down modestly. She hoped he would kiss her again. Yet at the same time, poor Joe was ill, and needed her. But a kiss meant nothing, did it? Only that he found her attractive, which was nice . . . He said suddenly, 'Let's walk for a while before dinner.'

'I'd love to.' The wine had relaxed her and she felt, as Adam did, that the atmosphere outside was more private and they could speak more easily. They walked along the path that edged the square dock and his hand moved lightly to her shoulders, rested casually there. She allowed it, trying not to wonder what it might lead up to. They stood at the chain railing, looking across at the museum, where life-sized models of dockers in period dress leaned over bales and barrels. And as they stood she allowed herself to put her own arm around his waist very lightly, her wrist resting on his hip-bone. His body was firm and slim, and the closeness of it aroused feelings she had only been dimly aware of before.

There were couples wandering along in the dim light,

the autumn air suddenly kind, and strangely warm for October. It seemed suddenly very natural for Adam to turn to face her, so that their arms encircled each other, to bend and kiss her with a new and wonderful sweetness. For a moment she remembered Joe—but there was no time for memories, only the physical joy of the present.

He drew away suddenly. 'I shouldn't—I'm sorry.'

Deflated, she said, 'Why not?'

'I didn't tell you, Sasha. I ought to have told you about my wife. She—died—almost five years ago. It was almost unbearable to watch her dying, and trying to stay cheerful for my sake.' He stared out at the opposite side of the square of dark water, and his eyes were seeing into the past. Sasha moved close to him, so that he could feel the warmth of her body. He said, 'I don't know yet if I have forgotten her—if it is fair to kiss you when it might be only my loneliness reaching out to you.' He turned to face her. 'Somehow, Sasha, there was something—serene—about you that appealed so much to me. I shouldn't allow myself to forget your innocence, and burden you with my problems.'

She said softly, 'Sometimes you don't seem all that much older than me, after all.'

'Oh, Sasha——' And she saw in his eyes a raw need, and it filled her with a great joy because she was the one he had turned to. And she knew she had enough gentle compassion and affection for him to help him get over his grief. The kiss that followed was deep and long and passionate. Yet no more words were spoken about it.

They walked on, the moments of intimacy over, but filled with a sense of closeness and understanding. Sasha treasured it, not wanting to speak in case she lost the feeling, as though she knew it was transitory and would not last. She was right. They went into the restaurant close by the river, the smell of the estuary's salt water drifting in through the door as the commissionaire welcomed them—clearly recognising

Adam. They sat down and ordered steaks. It was the end of their secret. He said, 'Now, tell me how Primary is going.'

'I'm not complaining. I've got a reasonable memory.'

'Which muscle has a U-shaped insertion? What are the main vessels in the brain? How long would I survive if my jugular vein was severed?' He fired questions at her with a rapidity which surprised her, but which she managed to answer. They both laughed as he ran out of questions. 'On the strength of that viva, Dr Norton, I hereby offer you a job in my department.'

She was still smiling as she said, 'I won't hold you to that. It will be four years before I'm ready.'

'I'm not joking,' he said quietly, his voice precise and sincere. 'You know your stuff. In four years you'll have the experience. I meant it.'

'Thanks, Adam.'

'Always providing you come up to the department at every opportunity, to see how we work.' He grinned.

She thanked him again. 'Let's get the exam over first. I still have to satisfy a few other people.'

'Fair enough.' And as the steaks were brought he said, 'And now, I'd better give you the low-down on Zaramos—that's why we're here, after all.' He began to describe the bay of Zaramos. By the time he had finished, she was almost hungry again at the sound of the fresh mullet and kebabs served up at the local taverna. She could see the wooden jetty in her mind's eye, and the fishing-boats, the open taverna with its smiling host Giorgios and his plump wife Maria. She could almost see the twinkling lights on the millionaire's yacht out at anchor in the bay, and taste the ouzo that flowed at ridiculously cheap prices. 'It isn't hard to find the villa. When you get off the ferry, turn left and follow the only road on the island. Stop when you come to the third house. Ask any goat. There is bound to be a large Persian cat sitting in the porch. His name is Emperor, and if he likes you he won't bite your leg off.'

They walked by the water again on the way back to

the car. This time they did not touch, as though they didn't need to—as though they both understood where their feelings were leading them, and felt afraid of any further commitment just then. The evening had been very sweet, in spite of knowing that his wife was still in his thoughts. They had got on well—like real friends. It was very early to be sure of anything, but she had a feeling inside her that she knew could very easily blossom into very real, outright love.

He drove her back through deserted Toxteth. 'Where do you live, Adam?'

'In the Albert Dock.'

'Truly? One of those luxury flats?'

'Yes,' he owned. 'I thought it—tactless to take you there tonight.'

'Of course.' She agreed with him. He had been open about his loneliness tonight. He had lived a very private life for many years, and she knew it would take more than one night with a sympathetic SHO to unlock Adam's deepest feelings. She was glad they had shared that one evening.

He parked under the ragged sycamore. 'Well? Have we covered everything you wanted to know? About Zaramos, I mean?'

'Yes—thank you for everything.'

'I'll be very offended if you start all this thanking business.' His hands went round her shoulders and he squeezed them. 'This has been a rather special day for me.'

'Me, too.'

They both knew why. They faced each other in the shadowy light from the one street-lamp in the car park and the single naked bulb in the porch of the doctors' residence. The wind had started up, so that the branches of the bare tree made flickering patterns on the damp ground. There was no sound but the whispering of the wind. She mouthed her goodnight, but before she had said it he had caught her tight against him. 'I've said far too much already,' he murmured into her hair. 'I'll see you before you leave. I'll let you know when I get the tickets.'

Adam released her, and Sasha nodded, not trusting herself to speak. She got out of the car and closed the door. She walked across the few yards to the porch, and opened her bag to get the key. She turned to look at the shadowy outline of the car. Adam was outside, coming towards her. She waited. The wind was noisier now, but she heard his words. Simple, normal words. 'I hope it isn't too late for you.'

'Not a bit.'

'I have a list in the morning.'

They were talking without purpose, at random, because neither of them wanted the evening to end. She said, 'Pat Moore is very good, isn't he?'

'Excellent. But I mustn't leave too much to him.' The wind gusted, and he said, 'Here, I'll move round to keep the wind from blowing you about.'

'I don't mind it.' Helplessly she looked at him, knowing she could never be the first to say goodnight. She put her hair out of her eyes, but it blew back again almost at once. Through the wildness of the wind a cargo vessel on the river gave a low hoot, the wind carrying the sound so that it sounded almost on top of them. 'The tide must be in.'

'I can see the ships from my window. Triple glazing, fortunately.' Adam smoothed back his own hair. He said reluctantly, 'I suppose I ought to let you go in.'

'I'm fine. Thanks again for getting the tickets for us.'

'I'm only glad the place will be aired—and Emperor have some company.'

'Your friend—Andreas—he won't mind having two girls to look after?'

Adam smiled. He had to raise his voice against the wind. 'He's Greek, Sasha—he'll do anything for a pretty girl.'

'Will it be warm? It's hard to imagine.'

'The Greek islands can be fickle. Take something warm, but hope for the sun.'

'I will.'

It had started to rain now, and as it grew heavier Adam said, 'This is ridiculous. Run in, now, and get out of those wet things. Better have a shower before you go to bed. Goodnight, Sasha.'

He gave her a push, and she felt suddenly responsible for him getting soaked, and opened the door. She forced her reluctant feet inside, where she squelched hurriedly up so that she could see him from the window. But the Rover was gone when she got inside, and she turned despondently to switch on the light. Then she screamed. She had forgotten that Joe had a key. 'What are you doing here?'

His voice was hard and strange. 'Making sure that lecher didn't come in with you.'

'Joe—I know you mean to be kind . . .' Troubled, she looked at him, praying for the right words. She was angry with him for being there, but understood that he might have problems. She took a step towards him.

With a swift movement he hit her in the face, so that she reeled back and fell at his feet, her hands over her face. 'I love you, you whore—I love you and you treat me like dirt!' And he aimed another blow into the air with a strangled sob, before rushing out of the flat and down the stairs, leaving the door wide open, until the wind banged it closed.

Sasha levered herself up to one elbow. She heard Joe's footsteps running swiftly away until they were lost in the noise of the gale. Then she put her hand to her face, and took it away stained red with blood.

CHAPTER FOUR

SASHA was woken by the telephone. She stirred, and wondered why she felt stiff and her head ached. She lifted the receiver. It was Sister from AED. 'Very sorry to wake you, Doctor, but there's been a pile-up on the M62, and we're expecting some of the ambulances to be diverted here. It was frosty early on.'

'I'll be there.' Sasha looked at the watch by her bed, feeling the pain in her eye as she turned her head. It was six in the morning—and she had only fallen asleep at two, distressed and disturbed by last night's events. She stood up slowly. Her face ached along the right side, and she thought over the number of battered women she had cared for in Casualty. And now she herself came into that category. If she had her way, she would hide her bruised face until it healed, never mentioning it to anyone. But she was on duty and, battered though she was, she had work to do.

She showered and dressed, and boiled the kettle for a quick coffee. What story would she give the staff? And how many of them would believe her? It was bad enough to see a doctor with a purple eye—purple, green and yellow, she decided as she studied it in the bathroom mirror—but when most of them knew that it must have been done by the man who possessed her front door key, it began to present moral questions she hadn't before faced. She realised that when she had seen these women she had automatically assumed that they must have irritated their men in some way. Now she saw clearly that some men were just cruel, unable to express themselves any other way than by violence. How very easy it was for a man to ruin a woman's reputation.

There was no point in asking for an eyepatch. That

would only draw even more attention. Dark glasses would hide it—but then she couldn't do her job. Taking a deep breath, she walked quietly into Casualty in a freshly laundered white coat, and went straight to the office. Sister Holloway looked at her. 'Good lord, woman, are you sure you can handle this?' Sasha assured her that she was fine. Sister jabbed a thumb in the direction of cubicle one. 'There are three with bruises and shock, but they seem to be in one piece.'

'OK.' There was an advantage in being busy—no one had any time to comment on Sasha's face. She went to the first casualty, a young man with a very bloody face, which the nurse was cleaning as gently as she could. Sasha examined him. 'I think these minor cuts will heal, but I'm going to have to stitch this long one. Did you go through your windscreen?'

'My own fault, Doc. Didn't bother with my seat-belt. Go ahead, let's get it over.' She saw him eyeing her as she gently drew the ends of the skin together, suturing as fast and efficiently as she could. When she had finished she praised him for not making a fuss, and he said, 'I'm OK, luv, but I hope the devil that did that to you gets his come-uppance, I really do.'

She smiled, the answer already in her mind, and helped him as he tried to stand up, groggily at first, but then more steadily. 'You mustn't curse the kitchen cupboard door like that.' And she left the nurse taking care of him as she went to the next cubicle. There was a handsome black girl leaning back against the pillows in a sitting position. 'Good morning. I'm Dr Norton. Where are you injured?'

The girl stared with frightened eyes. 'Me boyfriend, Doctor? Is he here?'

'I'll try and find out for you. I think the ambulances went to the Royal first. The clerk will find out for you, don't worry.'

'But some of them as went to the Royal was dead!'

Sasha looked at her with compassion. 'I'll ask, as soon as I've seen to you. What's his name?'

'Brooks—Gary Brooks.'

Sasha called a junior. 'Ask the clerk about a Gary Brooks, please.' She turned back to her patient. 'Now, anything hurting?' She quickly examined the girl's chest, and looked into her eyes.

'Only me shoulder when I lie down.'

'Here?' Sasha prodded the scapula. It appeared intact.

'It's not sore now.'

Sasha said, 'Lie down,' and helped her shuffle down to lie flat. As soon as she was down, she sat up again. 'Ow, that hurts!' She gripped her shoulder and grimaced.

Sasha called the nurse to make her comfortable in a sitting position. 'I think you might have some internal bleeding that's catching a nerve. Keep still, and I'll get a surgeon to see you.' The look of fright came back into the girl's beautiful eyes and Sasha said gently, 'Don't worry. I'll be here, and we should soon have news of Gary.' She went out to ring the surgical registrar, but he was already in the department, knowing he would be needed. Sasha called to him. 'I think this girl may have ruptured her spleen. She'll need a GA so you can explore the whole area.'

The young registrar smiled. Sasha had forgotten about her own eye, but he said, 'Right you are, Dr Norton. You look as if you've been in a crash, too.'

Her reply came off pat. 'No, just an argument with a kitchen cupboard.'

The registrar paused on his way to the cubicle. 'Aggressive sort of furniture you have, Doctor.' And he winked before pulling aside the curtain and going to the girl, Lily Campbell. He admitted her to the ward, and Sasha made sure the clerk knew where she was in case news of Gary should come through. Each line of enquiry had drawn a blank so far. Poor Lily—Sasha prayed that she didn't have to take bad news to the girl.

A nurse appeared at Sasha's side with a cup of tea. 'Dr Mortimer said you were to drink this before you do anything else.'

'Thanks, Julie.' That was wise of Philip. No one was any good in this department if they passed out on the job. 'I didn't get any breakfast.'

The nurse said hesitantly, 'Was it Joe Acourt did that to you?'

Sasha couldn't say yes or no. In that moment of hesitation, the nurse read the truth. Sasha said hastily, 'By accident, Julie. He doesn't know his own strength.'

Julie nodded sympathetically. 'He's been real funny lately. The girls in Physio say they don't know whether he's going to be nice to them or wipe the floor with them. You don't think he's going mental, do you? I mean—to do that to you, it——'

Sasha interrupted. 'Let's get back to work, shall we?'

The young nurse nodded. 'Sorry, Doctor.' But at that moment Barbie Green came into the department, and Julie scurried away.

Barbie said, 'Sasha! I heard you went out with Adam Harrington last night.'

Sasha hissed, 'Keep your voice down. I don't want the whole hospital to know.'

'The whole hospital does know. Better hide that eye. It was Joe, wasn't it? He's turning into an animal, Sasha—you can't go on like this.' She lowered her voice to a whisper. 'But you did enjoy going out with Adam? Was he as lovely as everyone says?' And for a moment Sasha remembered last night, and nodded, recalling the warmth of being intimately close, lovingly treated . . .

A loud, harsh ringing noise intruded into her reminiscences. The arrest button! At once the staff went into their well-rehearsed routine. Sasha's cubicle was empty, and the patient was rushed in, pale and sweaty. Philip Mortimer joined her and they examined the patient together. Philip said, 'I don't think it's cardiac. Just take a look into his eyes.' He handed the torch to Sasha, who nodded in agreement. Philip said, 'I'll call the neuro registrar.'

Pat Moore came down. 'Yes, better get him up to our

place. Adam is in theatre just now, but I'll get his opinion as soon as I can.' He called the porters to transfer the patient up.

Philip took Sasha's arm. 'I need a large breakfast. Coming?'

She looked up at the corridor clock and grinned. 'We might have to settle for lunch. But yes, I'm starving!' On the way she chatted about Gary Brooks, grateful that Philip didn't mention her black eye. They went to the mess and helped themselves to bacon and eggs and coffee. As they sat down Sasha noticed a group of surgeons still in theatre gear coming in for a quick snack. Her heart lurched as she recognised Adam, and she kept her back to him, chatting in a determinedly cheerful way to Philip Mortimer. The thought of the motorway crash was still very much with them, and she teased Philip about his Porsche. 'You would never speed when there's frost about, would you?'

'Perish the thought.' He grinned and cut a slice of fried bread. 'You know I only bought the thing to boost my shy, retiring image. Just a sheep in wolf's clothing, I am.' And as she dutifully laughed at that he said, 'Sasha, which car would you most like to own? I want to read into your character, and cars say a lot about their owners. Which make?'

She smiled again. 'One with four wheels would do nicely.'

At that moment the quiet voice of Adam Harrington cut into their conversation like a sweet sword, sending all thought from Sasha's head. His grey eyes went straight to Sasha's bruised eye. 'Pat Moore told me.'

'It's nothing—just an argument with a cupboard door.' But she saw in his face such compassion and concern that tears collected and threatened to spill over. To save herself, she asked about the patient who had just been taken up.

Adam said, 'I'll be operating in a few minutes. There's intracranial bleeding, and they're prepping him now. Come up later and see him.'

Philip seemed to assume that the invitation was for Sasha. She said, 'Thanks—we will if there's any free time.'

'Good—see you later then.' As he left them Sasha knew there were covert stares from the other occupants of the mess. Adam didn't seem to mind, but she felt herself the centre of all eyes.

She looked across at Philip, who was calmly finishing his last fried egg. 'I only went out with him last night—an innocent dinner—what's wrong with that?'

Philip allowed his attention to wander from his plate. 'He's a nice bloke—but he breaks hearts. Not the settling-down type, you see—can't get over his wife.' He shrugged. 'Like me, he suffers from being available. We have to accept that we're always being talked about. I'm the wicked-wolf type whom nobody expects to settle down. Adam Harrington is quieter—but, believe me, he leaves a trail longer than I do.' His voice softened for a moment. 'Kid, everyone sees you as totally innocent, and therefore unable to cope with being—well—dumped. Don't let him get to you, OK? Then we'll all sleep easier.'

Sasha smiled. 'I'll remember.'

'Right—keep cool. Laid-back. Then you'll survive the golfish-bowl existence with as much suavity as I do.' He stood up. 'Let's go up and watch Harrington operate. Pull the cap down low, and the mask up high, and no one will notice the periorbital haematoma.' He winked and led the way to the lift.

The theatre in Neuro was full of strangers visiting Adam. Sasha positioned herself where she could see his hands, and as the patient was brought in Adam began a simple commentary as he worked. Some angiograms had been done, and lay where he could refer to them. The shaved skull was exposed and he began to drill carefully. As expected, there was a burst of blood from the wound, and the blood pressure fell dramatically. Sasha forgot her obsession with the operator, and watched only his skilled hands as he and the anaesthetist worked fast to save a life. They found the source of the bleeding at last, and Adam forgot to speak as the remaining blood was sucked from the site and he tied the ends of the ruptured vessel. There was no sound but the suction and the machine breathing for the patient. There was a general sigh of relief in the theatre as the skull was replaced, and the flap of skin brought forward and stitched into place.

Her first thought was to get back to work. But as Sasha left the theatre Adam caught up with her. 'Well? You think you'd like to do that?'

She nodded. 'I would. I've always found surgery fascinating. But to operate in such a sensitive area—that must be most satisfying, even though more dangerous.' She saw that his visitors were waiting, and whispered, 'Adam, they want to speak to you.'

'They can wait. I want to know why he hit you.'

'He—saw us last night.' She hated having to give Joe away, but knew that Adam had a right to know. 'I know it can't go on. When I figure out how to do it, I'll intervene in some way—get him to see Dr Slade or something. But not now—'

'And not you. Sasha, you're too close, don't you see? It will have to be someone less involved with him. I——' But Pat Moore took his arm, and Adam realised this wasn't the place to talk. 'I'll catch up with you, Sasha.'

She made her escape, conscious of the looks and the stares. She knew she was being labelled Harrington's latest conquest. The looks were sympathetic, as though everyone knew what would happen to her. But she couldn't help what people thought. And she knew herself incapable of refusing him. He was like a drug she had only sampled once, but knew that she must have more, that she had no defence against him.

She was bleeped as soon as she arrived back in Casualty. Barbie was on the phone. 'I'm terribly busy, Sasha, but when can we talk?'

'I'll talk, but not about Joe, Barbie.'

'About last night?'

'Barbie, don't ask. Adam will get our tickets, that's all. But please don't go on at me about Adam. Nothing happened, if that's what you want to know.' Nothing, except getting to know a very special man who would be a hard act to follow . . .

'OK. I understand, Sasha. And I can't wait till December.'

'I'm looking forward to it, too.'

'I'll be in the common-room later.'

'See you then.'

She went back to work. It was strange that being in love gave all of life so much more colour and excitement. Even though Adam wasn't the settling-down type, he still made the Western Hospital the best place in the world to be. Sasha saw a suspected ulcer, and a woman who had lost weight but not told anyone about it until it was too late . . . She remembered to ask Sister about the lost Gary Brooks too. Lily was in the ward, waiting for surgery for her ruptured spleen. The day had almost gone, and the empty corridors seemed to lead nowhere, echoing, and vacant of all feeling, all joy, all comfort.

Sasha went to the phone outside the common-room and rang home. 'Hello, Mum.'

'Darling, how nice to hear you! Life treating you well?'

Sasha smiled and tried to be honest. 'I'm happy here. Work is fine, and my studies are going well. I've applied to do my Primary in Edinburgh in January. How's school?'

'My five-year-olds are manageable—but your father is having problems with his fourth form. They're all so aggressive these days.'

'How's William?' Her brother had always been distant—involved with things like sport and Outward Bound and camping in the snow.

'Doing well in Upper Sixth.' Her mother's voice changed. 'I was wondering if you might be home for

Christmas.'

'That's why I rang. I'm going to Greece with a friend—girlfriend."

'Greece? Met a millionaire, have we?'

'Not quite. It's one of our senior consultants—he isn't using his villa, so Barb and I can have it free.'

'Lovely—send us a postcard.'

'You're making me feel guilty now.'

'Darling, don't. I do know how hard you work. We'll see you when you can make it—and have a marvellous time.'

'I will. I love you, Mum.' She put the phone down and walked into the common-room, her thoughts still in the Pennine village where her family lived their simple, hard-working lives. No point in worrying them about Joe and his problems. No one could do anything about that but Sasha herself. Dear Joe—when she had first met him he'd been like a wonderful, kind elder brother, always there when she'd needed him, all cheerfulness and concern . . .

'Sasha.'

She turned to see Adam, the only occupant of the room. 'You shouldn't——'

'It's a free common-room,' he said drily, and she blushed scarlet at her assumption that he had come to see her. He was neatly dressed now, in his three-piece suit—respectable grey with a white shirt and university tie. It was slightly surprising that he was alone tonight, instead of leading his retinue of acolytes.

Sasha felt foolish. 'I've boiled the kettle if you want coffee, but I'm not sure if the cups are clean, and——'

'Shut up, Sasha.'

She stopped, turned and faced him. His voice softened as their eyes met. 'Don't waffle, darling, and tell me exactly what happened.'

He was taking over. Suddenly she remembered all she had been told that day about women whose hearts had been broken. She didn't want to be the last in a long line. Sasha Norton didn't really think she had the nerve to do it, but suddenly she did. 'I'd rather not, Adam.'

'But I have to know.'

She faced him, with a sudden feeling of strength. 'No, Adam—it's my problem, my affair. Just forget you ever saw me like this. It will fade in a few days.'

He took a step towards her. They were now close enough for her to feel the warmth of his body, smell the special masculine smell that was Adam. His eyes caught hers. 'Forget? How do I do that?' There was so much fire and passion in his eyes at that moment that it was the hardest thing she had ever done to turn away from what she longed for. He said, 'Well? How can I, Sasha?'

She steeled herself and clenched her fists. With the hotness of tears already stinging her eyelids, reminding her of the bruises round one eye, she said, 'I must go. Goodnight, Adam.' She strode out of the room and along the corridor. She didn't realise which direction she was walking in until she found herself in the physiotherapy department. It was deserted, except for one lone cleaner, who looked up from her vacuum cleaner with amazement, her glance locked on to the black eye. Sasha smiled suddenly at the expression on the woman's face. 'It's nothing. Just slipped in the kitchen.'

'I'll say it's nothing, queen. 'Ere, I'd give 'im what for if I was you. There's laws about things like that.'

'Easier said than done, Elsie.'

'Us women 'ave rights, you know.'

'I agree.' Rights. Sasha sighed, and stared round the empty department. This was where Joe worked, where he was king. Poor Joe. Yet as she caught sight of her own reflection in a mirror she thought for the first time, poor Sasha. Battered in body—and in mind, as she fought against her inevitable infatuation with Adam Harrington. Sasha plunged her hands deep in the pockets of her white coat as she tramped wearily to the main entrance and made her way across the chilly car park. She held her head higher as she walked, feeling herself walking away from Adam's fatal attraction, freeing herself from his spell.

There was a rustle behind her. She turned, but saw nothing in the twilight. She began to walk again, but the thought of the prowler loomed large in her mind. She knew she need not fear—Joe had given her and some of the other housemen lessons in self-defence. But to have to put them to use in real life was something she had never yet faced, and didn't want to. She walked more quickly. Then a voice called, 'Sasha, is that you?'

'Oh, Barbie, thank goodness! I must be getting jumpy in my old age.'

Her friend ran up, an old sheepskin jacket over her white coat. 'I looked in the common-room. There was only Adam sitting in the corner like an elegant ghost, all alone. He told me he's seen you—and about getting the tickets for us. I wonder why he was all alone?'

Sasha tried not to think of him. She had seen his raw loneliness, knew how he couldn't rid himself of the memory of his wife. To think of him sitting in the shadows alone brought back the feelings she had tried to squash. 'I think he was a bit worried about my black eye.'

'We all are. Did Joe just lash out? Or did he do it on purpose? I honestly can't see him ever wanting to hurt you.'

Sasha shook her head. 'Me neither. He sort of lashed out when I went to him—like an animal at bay.' She sighed. 'I just went to his department, but I didn't ask any questions. He'd just hate it if he thought I was snooping.'

They had reached Barbie's door, and she opened it and drew Sasha in after her. 'You looked after me, Sasha. Now it's my turn. Come and sit down for a while, and tell me how you feel.'

Sasha sat down without being asked. 'Terrible.'

Barbie was putting the kettle on. 'Did Adam kiss you last night?' A warmth spread through Sasha's body as she remembered last night. Kisses—she remembered them all and longed for more. Somehow, while he was kissing her, she was filled with a total joy and vitality, total happiness in a strange way; as though all else didn't matter. She didn't hear Barbie repeat her question as she remembered the way they had not been able to leave each other, had not wanted to say goodnight.

Barbara looked over her shoulder, busy with the teapot, and said nothing. Outside, the darkness and the fog thickened. She left Sasha to her own thoughts for a while. Then she said, 'What happens if we're all called out? It's thick fog outside.'

'They'll send a porter for us.'

'I see.'

Sasha looked up. 'Barbie, I'm sorry—dreaming away here. Tell me how you are. How's the depression? You seem better.'

They thought they heard a shout outside, and both went to the window, but could see nothing through the fog. Then Sasha's bleep went, and she took the phone. 'Dr Norton.'

'Sister Holloway, Doctor. A woman has been attacked. Not hurt, just terrified. I'm sending Jim to fetch you.'

'Right, Sister.'

Barbara said, 'Take my coat.' She put it round Sasha's shoulders as the porter came across to escort her. She let Jim in. 'Is the patient all right, Jim?'

'Crying, hysterical, but no bones broken.'

'OK, let's hit the road, Jim.' They tramped together, the fog masking every sound, until they saw the welcome brightness of the hospital doors. The patient was sitting in the cubicle, an untouched cup of tea at her elbow, her head bowed on her chest, a cheap coat wrapped round her. She was middle-aged, with dyed blonde hair. Sasha touched her shoulder. 'I'm Dr Norton. What happened?'

'I won't have to go to the police, will I?'

'Not if you've told our security people what happened.'

The woman began to sob again. 'He just grabbed me from behind. I didn't hear him coming. Big man. Sort of twisted me and tripped me up so I fell down.' Her pale eyes were ringed with red. She pulled up her skirt wordlessly and showed where the top of her thigh was red and scratched.

'And then you shouted, and the security men came?'

'Yeah.'

Sasha's heart was thumping, and she knew it was because she suspected that it might have been Joe. 'Did you get a look at him?'

'No. Only that he was wearing an anorak—one of them parka things. And a woolly hat.'

Sasha finished her physical examination. 'Would you like something to help you sleep?'

'Thanks, Doctor. Can I go home?'

'We'd like to keep you in overnight, if that's OK?'

'Thanks, Doctor. I'd feel safer here.'

The patient accompanied Sasha to Sister's office, where she was given a sedative. She was just about to be taken to the ward when a big black man pushed open the main doors. He was wearing a woollen hat and an anorak over jeans. The woman screamed, 'That's him!'

The man looked at her in surprise. He didn't look aggressive. In fact, he looked very worried. Sasha went to him. 'Can I help you at all?' Her heart was still banging away, knowing that Joe often wore a parka.

The man replied in a strong Liverpool accent. 'It's me girlfriend. They told me she was brought in 'ere. Lily, her name is—Lily Campbell. 'Ave you seen 'er, Doctor?'

Sasha felt a great sense of relief. 'You must be Gary.'

'Yeh, Gary Brooks—Lily's in 'ere? Is she all right?'

Sasha nodded, seeing the dark face brighten. 'She's all right, Gary. She needed an operation, but she's going to be fine. I'll ring the ward and see if you can visit, shall I?'

'Cor, thanks, Doctor.' And the big man's eyes filled, and he turned away to hide his weakness. 'I was just let out of the Royal. I got a taxi—took me last quid, but it was worth it.'

The woman who had been attacked shouted when she saw Gary being allowed in, 'But it was 'im! He attacked me!'

'I swear I didn't. Ask the taxi—see, he's still there. He's only just dropped me off.'

As Gary went upstairs to the ward Sasha left two pound coins with the Sister. 'That'll get him home tonight.' She turned to Jim. 'Well, if you'll walk me back, Jim—that attacker might be out there still, and I'd be glad of your company.'

Jim said, 'You seem awful sure that bloke didn't hurt that woman.'

'Jim, he's just out of hospital himself—worried sick about his girl. A man like that wouldn't attack another woman.'

'The trouble with you, Doctor, is that you're just too trusting. Just because you know Gary's name, doesn't mean he's innocent, you know.'

Too trusting . . . Yes, perhaps she was. But she wasn't stupid, and although she might fall in love too easily she wasn't so easily deceived in human nature. Yet Joe—she had never read violence in his blue eyes, but it had surfaced in his nature. 'Oh, Jim, life is odd sometimes. I don't want to go round suspecting everyone.'

'Too right. But these days you can never tell.' Jim was a pessimist at the best of times. 'Even your best friend could be a rapist—you read about them all the time, being just ordinary folks with girlfriends and mothers and that.'

'Yes, Jim—I suppose you do.' Sasha's heart was as cold as the fog.

CHAPTER FIVE

NOVEMBER advanced with its usual grim foot-steps. The hospital was gloomy, the lights dim by order of the health authority, who were demanding economies in all directions. It made the dreary corridors even drearier, and for a while made Barbie's depression come back. Only in town did the big stores try to drag the city into a festive mood, by outdoing each other with gaudy decorations.

Sasha dragged Barbie into town, mainly to get her out of the hospital, but also to look among the woollies and shawls and furs for last-minute cottons for the beach and the tavernas. They stood in Dolcis, staring at rows of boots.

'Adam warned us to take warm things as well,' said Barbie.

'Well, you can't wear boots on the beach.'

'What if it's cold and wet?'

Sasha took her firmly by the arm and led her to a café where she ordered espresso coffee. 'This is what we'll be drinking out there. Can't you just imagine the white beaches and blue water?'

Barbie's mood lifted slightly. 'And the green olive groves and the black goats.' She paused thoughtfully. 'I've never seen a black goat. Dad kept goats, but they were all white.' She looked across the table. 'Thanks for getting me out. I'm terribly sorry to be a bore.'

'You'll get over it.'

Barbie said, 'That eye of yours is finally back to normal, anyway. Have you seen Joe since it—happened?'

Sasha shook her head. 'Only in the distance. I think it shook him, knowing I was walking around and everyone was guessing it must be him. Poor Joe,' she added, still feeling a sense of loss for the man she used to know a long time ago. 'This Joe just isn't the real one.'

They went back to the Western after a lunch of baked potatoes in the Orchard Tea Rooms in Church Street. Already in mid-afternoon, dusk was falling, and the hospital windows were lit up in the grey street, with bare trees standing black and lonely against the frosty sky. They crossed the car park, skirting the frozen puddles— only to see a man coming out of the residence. Barbie spotted him first. 'Isn't that Adam?'

He recognised them and strode to meet them. 'I just brought the tickets.'

Sasha looked up at him, thrilled as she always was to be near him, and the dank afternoon vanished and the sun came out for her. 'Would you—er—like a cup of tea?'

'I'd love one.' Adam didn't hesitate. And as they went up the stairs she told herself that, rich and famous though he was, it was still a grey November Saturday afternoon, and he was alone.

Over tea in the kitchen, where it was warmer, Adam produced not only their air tickets, but also some photographs of Zaramos that showed a typical wooded island, with red-roofed houses and clean beaches washed by turquoise waves. 'And this one is my friend Andreas, who will be there if you need him.' Andreas was handsome, in a plump and jolly way, his curly black hair receding from his olive face. Sasha realised how young Adam looked for his age, with his abundant hair only tinged with silver over his ears a little.

Barbie took the next photograph. 'Is this his wife?'

Adam looked at it. 'His sister, Artemis. She's an artist.' Something in his voice made Sasha look at Adam before she looked at the girl. Then she knew why Adam Harrington didn't settle down with any of the women he took out in Liverpool. Artemis Daniacos was stunning, with big black eyes, a slim, graceful figure, and hair that rippled down her back to her waist. And Adam was staring at the picture with an expression of happy reminiscence that left Sasha feeling out in the cold. This lovely lady was surely more than a friend's sister to Adam; she must be first in line to fill his empty heart.

He looked up suddenly and caught her staring at him, and his smile was just as sudden, and full of perception, as though he knew what Sasha had been thinking. She smiled back, but felt a deep abyss growing wider and wider between them. She knew that she had secretly hoped that Adam Harrington might one day feel affection for her—but one look at that photograph had banished that hope forever. She had set her hopes too high. The existence of Artemis would remind her that someone as handsome and distinguished as Adam would surely never be happy with a simple SHO from the Pennines. How could she ever have allowed herself any such dreams?

At least, she told herself, this would put in perspective any joy she felt in his kisses, any delight in recalling the night they couldn't bear to say goodnight . . . It had been a sweet feeling, but now she knew it meant very little in Adam's scheme of things. She hid a sigh and sat back as she looked at the other photographs, feeling glad she had discovered his secret before she made a fool of herself.

Just then the doorbell rang and she excused herself to answer it. Please don't let it be Joe, she silently begged. His jealousy could flare up so quickly now, and it would be futile when there was absolutely no reason for jealousy. But when she opened the door it was young Gary Brooks who stood there, pathetic in his worn anorak and woolly cap. 'Gary! Is something wrong? Come on in, do. There's some tea in the pot.'

He hung back, hearing voices. 'No, Doctor—you've got visitors. Just a word, if it's orright.' He hunched himself by the doorpost.

'It isn't Lily, is it?'

'Oh, no, she's back 'ome. It's—well, the pigs—I mean the fuzz——'

Realisation dawned on Sasha. 'The police have been to see you? They think you are the prowler?'

'They've been to our 'ouse three times, Dr Norton. They ain't got nuthink on me, but they want to find somethink. Me mam's that upset.'

'But what can *I* do, Gary?'

'You never thought it wuz me, did you?'

Sasha shook her head. 'No. I think that woman was so upset that she screamed when she saw you only because you're coloured.'

Gary shrugged and heaved a great sigh. 'I've just gorra sort of face people think the worst of. I'm not that sort of bloke, honest.'

'And you want me to speak to the police? I don't know you very well, Gary. I can be a character witness, I suppose, but I haven't known you for long. I can only say I believe you didn't do it, that's all.'

Gary's face changed, his tensions vanished. 'I'll never forget it, Doctor! There's no one else I can get, you see. I never went to school that much—and I haven't gorra job.'

'I'll come along then, and meet your mother, shall I? Write down where you live, and I'll call and have a chat to your mother.' She knew she could pass this on to the social workers, but somehow it wouldn't mean the same to Gary. He wrote the address on her pad in the hall, then turned to go down the stairs, his shoulders hunched up against the world. She stood for a moment, wondering why life was so cruel to some people. Then she folded the paper with the address on it, and went into the kitchen to put it carefully in her purse.

Adam said at once, 'Is something wrong?'

She sat down at the table and refilled her cup. Thoughtfully she said, 'I'm only twenty-four. Yet I'm expected to deal with the problems of people from the saddest parts of humanity, to the most fortunate, and back again.' She shook her head. 'Why me?'

Adam said quietly, 'Don't ask. Just do what you can, and be glad you can help some of the people some of the time—especially in this city, where there are more have-nots than haves.'

Barbara said, 'I expect you know more haves—especially on Zaramos.'

He smiled. 'Andreas's father is a shipping millionaire. Spends a lot of time on his yacht. More time than he ought, but he used to be poor, so he still likes to show off.' He looked at his watch, and said, 'Oh, dear, I'm meeting someone. I must be off.' He looked at Sasha. 'Don't forget—people are people everywhere, and we all need help at times, even the most powerful. We're the lucky ones—we have something to give.' And he ran lightly downstairs and crossed the car park, turning once to wave as the girls stood at the window watching him.

Barbie said, 'That man has been a saviour to me.'

'He's a good man.' Sasha walked back to the table, her thoughts still preoccupied with the image of Artemis.

'I bet he never felt depressed when he was a houseman—probably just got on with the job. How I wish I could.'

Sasha tried to be cheerful. 'Just think, if you hadn't suffered your reactive depression, we might not be going to Zaramos.'

Barbara gave a secret look. 'He likes you, Sasha—even I can see that. I'm pretty sure that even if I weren't here, he would have found a way to get to know you.'

'I wonder.' Sasha washed the cups with an abstracted air, while Barbie looked at the tickets and the brochure and made little noises of appreciation at the beauty of the scenery they were promised in just a few short weeks.

They walked across to the mess for dinner, feeling too lazy to cook. The darkness was damp and full of mist and dew, and the few remaining leaves on the floor were wet and slippery. They were glad to get inside, even though the lights in the mess were dim and they could

53298
5280 &

490

53985

hardly see to eat their pizzas. They lifted their spirits by comparing their present meal with the feasts they intended to have on Zaramos. Barbie said suddenly, 'I say, isn't that Joe over there?'

Sasha turned. It *was* Joe, sitting alone with a cup of cold coffee, his head bowed and his expression blank. Sasha picked up her own coffee at once, followed by Barbie. 'Mind if we sit here, Joe?' she said quietly.

His face came to life as he looked up, and animation came into his eyes, eyes which had once twinkled permanently. 'I'd like that,' he said, his voice expressing all the regret and penitence Sasha could have asked for.

Barbie said, 'You look tired, Joe. Why don't you take a holiday? Come to Greece with us?'

'No way. No leave left. But thanks for asking me.'

They sat and chatted, their conversation stilted at first. But gradually a trace of the old Joe came back, thankfully with no sign of the jealousy or bad temper that had characterised their last few meetings. Sasha said, 'Why don't you come back to our place and we can play some music?'

And her heart pained at his eager expression as he said, 'Are you sure?' and looked at her, his blue eyes touchingly vulnerable.

'Yes, definitely. I'm not studying tonight.'

'That's great, then.'

Her one fear was that Joe might stay on after Barbie went to bed. But as they played folk music, Sasha carefully avoiding any smoochy numbers, or anything that might remind them of happier days together, Joe showed himself restrained and subdued. She wondered if anyone had perhaps spoken to him about hitting her—and she hoped they hadn't. But it was a subject neither of them could bring themselves to mention. When Barbie yawned and said she was tired it was Joe who stood up first and thanked them for having him. 'Nice to hear some good music. The wards are full of carols already.'

'Don't you like carols?' Barbie asked.

'I love them. But the nice warm feelings go away so quickly when Christmas is over.' Sasha began to hope that the illness of mind that had caused Joe's truculence and aggression was passing away at last. This evening he had been polite and gentle. Joe said, 'Thanks, both of you. Cheered me up no end.' And he waved, refusing to allow them to come and see him out. His smile at the door was almost as cheerful as it used to be.

'He's getting better, thank heaven,' said Barbie, as they watched him walk across the car park.

'Maybe.' Sasha's heart still ached for him. 'I could see he was hurting inside, Barbie—like you were when you first became ill. I wish I knew what I could do to help him.'

Barbie hugged her. 'You did it tonight. Just let's go on showing him that we've forgotten all the bad things.'

Sasha sighed. 'And remembered the good ones. We were so friendly at one time—I was really very fond of him when he made me laugh at myself, and when he taught us self-defence and that sort of thing. They were good times, Barbie.'

Barbie said thoughtfully, 'He couldn't really be the prowler, Sasha, could he?'

'I can't see Joe doing anything bad—yet look what he did to me.'

Barbie nodded. 'I shouldn't have mentioned it. 'Night, Sasha—let's just remind ourselves that there are only three weeks to go!'

'Before Zaramos? Yes . . .' And Sasha wondered if she would enjoy Zaramos as much as her friend would, now that they might meet the ravishing Artemis. Was Adam quite bowled over by her? Or had he known her as long as he had known Andreas, seen her blossom from a teenager into the beauty she was today? And did it make a lot of difference to his lonely existence, knowing that she was there, waiting to soothe and comfort his loneliness whenever he chose to visit her? Sasha remembered for the thousandth time the joy of being in his arms, of being held so tightly that she could scarcely get her breath—and the feeling of wanting to stay there for the rest of her life. Did Artemis feel that?

The following weekend, Sasha knew she must keep her promise to go and see Gary Brooks—he wouldn't dare to contact her again, and he must be waiting, feeling sure that she wouldn't come. She determined to go early, and caught the bus into Toxteth with mixed feelings, only knowing that she couldn't let him down. She got off in Parliament Street near to the cathedral, and stared at the blocks of new maisonettes that had replaced old run-down housing stock, surrounded with green grass and small new trees.

As she walked down Granby Street she was aware of numbers of eyes staring at her, recognising a stranger, and wary of her. Nervousness suddenly got the better of her and she darted into a small corner shop. Behind the till, a thin Muslim stared even harder at her, his sharp black eyes taking in every detail of her woollen jacket and tweed skirt over suede boots. She said, trying to be confident, 'Could you direct me to Culcheth Street, please?'

'Sure, luv,' came a broad Liverpool accent. 'First left—yer can't miss it. Nice weather fer ducks!' As she left the shop a group of youths got out of a Mercedes. They stared openly as she rounded the corner and came to the house she was looking for—small, neat, with lace curtains and a tiny lawn behind a wrought-iron gate.

She went along the narrow path, and knocked at the door. There was a pause, during which she knew she was still being watched. A black woman opened the door—small, plump, with a tense frown. 'Yes?' She looked resigned, as though she knew what was coming. 'Who is it that you want?' There was a Jamaican twang to her speech.

'Gary Brooks, please. I'm Dr Norton. I promised to call and see you.'

The woman's face was suddenly split by a broad smile. 'Hey, Doctor, come on in! You looks that young! Gary said you was a comin', but I sez to him that no doctor would want to come out 'ere.'

Sasha stood in the tiny hall, with a thick, gaudy carpet and pictures of the Pope on the wall. 'I said I'd come and see what I could do to help. I believe the police have been questioning you?'

The woman laughed, loud and high. 'That ain't nothink new.'

'You aren't worried?'

The smile vanished. 'Sure I am. But what good does worryin' do? I bet all them Nosy Parkers outside think you is a judy cop. But that's the way we live, Doctor, and there's no kindly visit goin' to change all that.'

Sasha said simply, 'I wish it could.'

The woman looked at her. Then she said quietly, 'Come on in, then—will you have a cup of tea?'

'Yes, please.'

'Gary's in his room.' She called up the narrow stairs, carpeted with the same bright pattern. Gary came out of a room, where loud reggae music issued after him, and gave a whoop as he recognised Sasha.

Over tea, Bella Brooks told her something of her life. Her stoic acceptance of a life far away from her beloved home in the sun bore no resemblance to the prevailing theory of immigrants coming here for their own benefit. Women like Bella were caught up in a larger web they had no way of controlling. Bella said, 'I know my Gary is good. Some of the fellas round 'ere—they run wild, man. I swear he never go with them. He an' Lily—they go to Blackpool to find work this summer. They on the way back—comin' home—when accident happen. Accident when you save our Lily's life, Doctor.'

'You mean they were in Blackpool during the summer?'

'Most of the time, yes. I tell the police, but they say because he come home two, three weekend, that he still suspect.'

Sasha shook her head, suddenly glad she had come. 'Oh, no, Mrs Brooks, he can't be a suspect. All the attacks were during the week. If he was away, then he's in the clear.'

It was Bella's turn to whoop with joy. 'So what we do, Doctor?'

'Just get a note from the hotel where they worked, confirming the dates they were there. Take it to the police, and say I sent you.'

After helping her draft a letter, Sasha stood up to go. Bella said, 'I'll walk along to the bus with you. Them cheeky boys, they might give you hassle.'

'It's all right, really. It's raining.'

'Rain is the least of my worries, Doctor.'

The two women walked along Granby Street together, both under Bella's umbrella, and Bella made no bones about shouting aloud if anyone dared to stare. 'Don't be so nosy, when I just takin' my friend to the bus stop!' She stood with her till the bus came. Then she said quietly, 'I just never thought you'd take the trouble.' And her tone was humble and grateful. Sasha went upstairs on the bus, because it was empty there, and no one would see the tears in her eyes.

It was almost holiday time, and Sasha had packed most of her things a week beforehand, leaving only clean towels and washing things for the last day. She had determined not to make a special effort to see Adam before they left. He had already given them the keys and details about where to get provisions for themselves. She packed her books into the bookcase. It would do her good to forget her studies for a while though before she went she remembered to send the fee to Edinburgh, so that they knew she would be sitting the Primary fellowship in January.

Then, the night before they left, her phone rang. It was Adam. 'Good luck on Zaramos.'

'It's very nice of you to ring.' Her heart had leapt at the sound of his voice, in spite of her determination not to allow such gymnastics any more. 'We can't wait to leave all this rain and cold behind us.'

'I wanted to ask, Sasha—did you go and see that young man's family?'

'I didn't think you would remember. Yes, I did. We sorted it all out. They won't have any more trouble—not about this case, anyway.'

'Tell me about it.'

'It's a long story.'

'I want to know.' His voice was quiet, unpushy, and she knew that Adam would understand her motives for going and trying to help. He wouldn't ridicule her concern. She told him what had happened. 'Go on,' he said.

'Well, that's all, really. I loved his mother—I'll never forget that look of patience and unselfishness in her eyes.' There was no answer for a moment, and she said, 'Adam? Are you still there?'

'Sasha, do you know what I think of you?'

Her heart thumped as she said, 'No—very ordinary, I suppose.'

He said, 'I'll tell you one day.'

'Not now?'

'No—I rang tonight to tell you one of my patients will run you to the airport. He always does it for me, and he'd be offended if I didn't ask him.'

'Thank you again. For everything.' She wanted to say more, but she never prolonged conversations with Adam, knowing how busy he was. 'See you when we get back.'

'Have a good trip.' The glib phrases could mean anything. Sasha put the phone down, and wondered when she would stop loving Adam Harrington. And what *did* he think of her? Was he really going to tell her one day? She flung her newly dried towels into the suitcase, and locked it. Then she wrote a label, reading 'Dr Norton, Zaramos, via Corfu.' And she smiled and went over it to make the letters darker.

Adam's grateful patient talked all the way to Manchester Airport about how wonderful Adam was. It was early in the morning and the motorway was almost empty, the sad winter fields on each side looking weary and tired. But as they neared Ringway the dawn lit up the wide expanse of sky with delicate pinks and yellows, and the sun rose in a burst of brilliance as they turned off towards the continental terminal. Barbie tried to give him some money—'Just for the petrol.'

But he refused it. 'You know how it is, Doctor,' he said. 'When you've been given your life back, then you want to spend the rest of your time showing the medical profession how much you appreciate what they've done for you.' And he gave them a little wave as he left their cases on a trolley. 'Have a wonderful holiday—you deserve it.'

Barbie watched him go. 'I'd never looked at it like that,' she mused. 'I see doctors as just ordinary people.'

Sasha smiled. 'Come on—you don't want to miss the plane, do you?' She thought she knew why Adam had sent them with that particular driver. The patient's gratitude was something Barbie hadn't had much of, and it might just remind her how lucky she was to have such a job, where people would remember you for life.

The airport was crowded with people with the same idea as them—to get away for Christmas. But their excitement didn't diminish as they stood in queues to check in, and more queues to get a cup of coffee. It was the first time either of them had flown, and to be going off to an exotic island was a joy that made their eyes shine and their pulses race. Only as they settled themselves in their seats and fastened their seat-belts did Barbie say, 'I wonder why Adam isn't going this holiday? He seems to think a lot of those friends he has out there.'

'That had occurred to me, too,' Sasha owned. 'Especially that glamorous Artemis.'

'Oh, I shouldn't worry about her, Sasha. She's probably married with a dozen kids.'

'I hadn't thought of that.' Sasha leaned back and smiled, the thought definitely improving the view of Zaramos even before they set foot on it.

The journey became less comfortable when they

alighted at the airport in warm, sticky Corfu and took
a crowded bus to the ferries. But their excitement
didn't diminish with each new fascinating aspect of their
trip, so that being loaded on the creaking wooden ferry,
along with crates of chickens, goats with tiny kids,
perspiring tourists like themselves, as well as peasants
with faces that looked two hundred years old, wizened
and creased by aeons in the Ionian sun, was nothing
more than the last thrilling adventure before their
holiday began in earnest. Barbie sat on the square
wooden seat as the boat waddled and swayed like a fat
old woman across the green sea towards the mysterious
islands and far out on the horizon, and gazed ahead like
some ancient explorer. 'Out there is peace, quiet and
warmth! Sasha, I think I'll stay on Zaramos! Liverpool
will just have to manage without me.'

Sasha poked at her as they neared the island.
'Look—a yacht. That must belong to Andreas's father,
the ship owner.'

They stared with round eyes at the white beauty
reflected in the still green waters like a graceful swan.
They couldn't read the name, as it was written in Greek,
but they could see a group of suntanned people sitting
on deck, a table with tall glasses between them, and hear
the lilt of Greek folk music coming from the yacht.
Barbie said, her voice an awed whisper, 'Do you think
we might one day be sitting like that? If Adam is
friendly with them, you never know!'

Sasha didn't answer as the ferry rounded the
headland and turned into the small picturesque
harbour, where the taverna they had seen on
photographs appeared close by the jetty where they were
to disembark, along with hundreds of chickens and a
group of pink English tourists. But only she had
noticed, just before they lost sight of the yacht, the slim,
graceful figure of a tall woman in a white dress, whose
long black hair hung down her waist. She wore
sunglasses, and walked like a goddess. Sasha muttered,
as they struggled to get their cases on the jetty without

hurting the chickens, 'She doesn't look as though she has a dozen kids!'

CHAPTER SIX

IT WAS not surprising that Sasha's thoughts about the lovely Artemis didn't spoil her holiday one bit. The girls' cases were taken at once by a smiling taxi-man, who said in broken English that Dr Andreas had told him to look out for the two ladies from Britain. Adam's villa was only half a mile from the jetty, and they were taken right to the gate, where a handsome, large grey Persian cat lounged in the dusk under a swathe of lavender that filled the air with sweetness.

'We're right on the beach, Sasha. Just look at that!' Barbie leaned on the gate and stared out at the twinkling lights of the boats in the bay, and up the opposite hill, where roofs peeped through dark green woodlands.

'I can hardly believe it,' breathed Sasha, kneeling to stroke the cat, which walked over to them with graceful interest, and condescended to purr when she stroked his lovely head. 'Hello, Emperor. I'm Sasha, and I've come to look after you for two weeks.' And the lovely creature blinked his large eyes, as though responding with equal politeness to her invitation, and purred louder.

After some time spent breathing in the new fresh scents, and gazing at the beauties of the island from the front gate, they decided to leave unpacking for now, to explore the villa, and then walk down to the taverna for a meal. Barbie said, 'I'm starving. I've been looking forward to eating there ever since Adam first described the landlady's cooking.'

'Let's see if there's any hot water. I'd like to change first.'

'All right, but only a quick shower—or you'll find me dead from starvation. What does the cat have to eat?'

From the bathroom Sasha called, 'It's in the cupboard marked with his name. And there should be some milk in the fridge left by the maid.' The water was warm, and she found a towel and clean dress from her suitcase to put on after her shower. She sighed with pleasure at just being warm, at not having to look for a cardigan or sweater, and at walking about in bare feet.

Barbie followed her in the bathroom. 'We might as well share this bedroom—it's huge. Gosh, Sasha, have you given a thought to the Western Hospital casualty department tonight?' She tried on a couple of skirts before deciding on the brightest scarlet one.

Sasha said firmly, 'No one is allowed to talk about work. That's why we're here, remember? I must say, your face doesn't show much sign of depression. Adam's medicine really works.'

Barbie sat on the bed to do her eyes. 'I wonder why Adam didn't come. It would have been nice to have a handsome escort to take us around and show us the olive groves and the goats.'

'You can't have everything in this life,' said Sasha, as she brushed her hair until it shone, and remembered that Adam had liked it down about her face . . . 'We'll enjoy finding our own way round. I hope you've got some tough shoes, because I'm going to the top of that hill tomorrow morning.' She pointed across the bay, where the slopes opposite were alive with lights, and the stars above the hill echoed the cheerful sparkle. 'I think there's a church right on top. Can you see, Barbie? It's floodlit. Oh, how beautiful!'

'What about sunbathing? Can't we get a tan first? I didn't know you were the active type, Sasha. I'm naturally lazy.' She bounced up and down on one of the single beds. 'I say, do hurry. I'll wait for you in the garden, I think. I want to stare at that yacht and imagine that we're on board, being served champagne by a tall, bronzed Greek with lots of money and oodles of charm.'

Sasha smiled, but didn't try to stop her friend, who

was obviously over-excited at being transported to Wonderland after the tough time she had been through during her first six months of housemanship. She hoped that the holiday would work, as Adam intended, and show her that life wasn't all hard work and no sleep. Sasha looked at herself critically in the long mirror. When she was relaxed, she owned that she was quite presentable, with her shining shoulder-length hair and dark brown eyes. She was taller than Barbie, and slim. Perhaps when she had time to think about her appearance more she might cultivate a slinky walk like Artemis, and maybe grow her hair? She smiled at the thought, and followed Barbie out into the soft, warm evening.

Emperor was hunting in the shadows, and the scent of the lavender was even sweeter now. It was tempting just to stand and allow her senses to be assailed on all sides by peace and beauty—but hunger was stronger than the call of beauty, and they set off at a brisk walk along the narrow coastal road towards the harbour. The jetty was quite crowded, and they hesitated just a little before descending the cobbled road into the bright lights of the village itself. The throng was mixed—holiday-makers rubbing shoulders with fishermen, and peasants side by side with sailors from the small flotilla which had sailed in that day, who were busy folding their gear before making their way to one of the tavernas.

'Tomorrow,' said Sasha, 'I'll buy some food and try to cook as they do here. The smell is overpoweringly delicious.'

'Well, there's definitely lots of garlic. And fish.' Barbie sniffed the air. 'Come on, we'll go to the taverna that Adam told us about. We know they speak English there. I don't want to order octopus or hedgehog without knowing.'

The landlord was busy serving at the bar. The girls walked through the main open-air front into a dining-room at the back, where small tables were covered with checked cloths, and a plump woman was serving meals.

At that moment a man detached himself from the bar with a bottle of wine and three glasses. 'So you are here at last! I am Andreas, and I have been waiting for you on the strict orders of my friend Adam.' He put the glasses down and shook hands with them both as they introduced themselves. 'I may buy you dinner? You prefer to be alone?'

Barbie said at once, 'No, we hate to be alone, Dr Andreas. We were hoping we would meet you. Adam has told us so much about you.' He was more handsome than his photograph—although his glossy hair was thin on top, it was luxurious and jet black elsewhere. His waistline showed evidence of good living, and his casual shirt was elegant and expensive. Barbie added, 'You are the local doctor here. You aren't on call, are you?'

Andreas's laugh was large and generous. 'Zaramos is small, Barbie. Wherever I am, someone will know. I dislike to think of myself as being on call. I prefer that they know the doctor will be available if he is needed. You will find life here most easygoing. That is why you are here, no? To unwind from all your coldness and your hard work?' He turned to Sasha. 'You are very quiet. You like the noise and the bustle when Greek people eat and drink?'

Sasha apologised for seeming distant. 'It's all so much fun, after the last few months in Liverpool. And I've been studying a lot—for my Primary. I do enjoy watching more than taking part.'

When the dancing started she insisted that she preferred to watch, and it was true. Barbie Green was a different person, as she watched Andreas show her the steps of the folk dances, and then entered into the spirit herself with a swirl of her scarlet skirt. The red Greek wine had made Barbie brighter, while Sasha found herself feeling sleepy. It had been a long day, yet she didn't want to spoil Barbie's fun by dragging her away.

When they paused by the table Sasha made her excuses, insisting on going home alone. 'If you're sure, Sasha.' Barbie clearly didn't want to leave yet—and why should she? Sasha wandered out into the air, still kind at almost midnight. Groups of fishermen were just putting out to sea, while flotilla sailors were continuing the party on board their boats. She walked slowly round the harbour, and then back along the quiet road towards the villa. It was an exquisite place, and she thought fondly of Adam Harrington for allowing them to enter his own private bolt-hole, to meet his friends and take possession of his home.

The first day set the pace for both girls. Sasha enjoyed going to sleep early and waking in the full flush of dawn to walk for miles among the trees and flowers. Barbie got up around midday, and they would meet in the evening for a meal at the taverna. When Andreas was there the second and then the third evening Sasha worried that Barbie might be getting stars in her eyes rather too soon. But she kept quiet then—surely her friend could take care of herself, and understood about holiday romances?

At the end of the first week, Andreas said over their grilled mullet, 'You must join us on Christmas Day. My father is giving one of his all-day parties, and my sister is coming from Athens.'

'On the—yacht?' Barbie's eyes were wide.

'On the *Dolphin*, yes.' Andreas smiled, and his smile involved his whole face, so that his eyes lit up and his chin dimpled. 'You have seen her in the bay? My father is planning some great apartment project all up the hillside, and right now he battles with the planners and the architects.'

Sasha said, 'Your sister—was she on board the day we arrived?'

'I believe she was.'

'I saw a woman in white as the ferry passed.'

Andreas nodded. 'Yes, that would be Artemis. She flies in at weekends quite often when she doesn't have a show. But in general there is a shortage of pretty women.' And his wide smile took in both girls.

Sasha said, 'You are not married, Andreas?'

Openly he said, 'No, not as such. But when I fly to New York on business, there is a lady surgeon there with whom I stay—and who I have been proposing to for the last four years. I think perhaps one day she will say yes.' He didn't seem embarrassed. 'It would be nice one day to settle down.' He poured more wine into each glass. 'Now, my friend Adam—he had a very happy marriage. I attended the wedding. No one knew that poor Deborah already had leukaemia. It was so very sad, because Adam was the kind of man who needed a happy home life—he wasn't one for dancing and drinking, as I am.' He paused, and went on quietly, 'I hope he stops grieving one day and finds someone to take Deborah's place. Is there no one in Liverpool he is fond of?'

Sasha looked down. Barbie didn't answer, so Sasha said, 'He seems very busy with his work. He entertains many visiting consultants.'

Andreas waved his arm. 'Oh, work, work! Anyone can work! What will he do when he wants to live, and finds that he is too old? I must speak with him again.' But he had spotted both girls' diffidence when Adam was mentioned, and when Sasha looked up she saw that he was still looking at her. She blushed at his gaze, and he seemed inwardly satisfied that his question had been answered.

She said firmly, 'He seems very fond of Artemis.'

He appeared to see her unspoken question. 'Adam has been my friend since we studied in London together, and my sister has been his friend almost as long. He could have married her then—but he chose Deborah. Why should he choose her now?'

She answered him with his own words. 'What will he do when he wants to live and finds he is too old?'

Andreas reached out and shook her by the hand. 'Well said, Sasha. Perhaps I must arrange for Artemis to be here next time Adam visits Zaramos?' And he pulled Sasha to her feet as the musicians began to play. 'Come, no excuses. You must learn the dance, now that your friend is an expert.' And Sasha made no complaint. She enjoyed dancing, and had watched them, so she knew the steps. When they returned to the table, breathless, her cheeks were flushed and her eyes shone. As Barbie got to her feet to join Andreas, he said quietly to Sasha, 'You need a partner, my little bird. You are living too little an existence. You must live while you are young. You have much to give.' And he twirled Barbie away, leaving Sasha to think over what he had said.

The next night was Christmas Eve, although, as the sun glowed lazily over the sea and made diamonds sparkle in the azure depths, it felt very little like it. Both girls lazed on the beach, knowing that the village would be alive with music and dancing and fireworks in the evening. Barbie spoke about her inner thoughts. 'I know this kind of magic is only temporary. Don't worry, I'm not being carried away. But we are so very lucky to be able to share this type of life—even if it's just for a week or so. I'll never be able to thank Adam for doing this for me—a silly little houseman he hardly knew.'

'So you feel able to go back to more of the same late nights and demanding patients and no sleep?'

'I'll finish housemanship, that's for sure. Then I'll take your advice and train for a nine-to-five job in school or industrial medicine. How about you? Still want to stay on that long, straight and narrow road until you make it to consultant surgeon?'

Sasha watched a seagull wheeling on still wings, wheeling and turning over the white shape of the *Dolphin*. It called shrilly as someone on deck threw it something to eat, then swept down and caught it in mid-air. 'I'll do it—for as long as I can. I'm still only at the first hurdle. That in itself seems ten feet high. So few people pass first time, you know. Oh, let's not worry about it today. Let's stick to our rules and not talk about work until we get back to it.'

'Excellent comment. What shall we wear tonight?'

'I'm wearing my dark blue. I'm walking up to that

tiny church on the hill for the midnight service.'

'I'll come, too. Andreas says most of the village goes there.' Barbie smiled at Sasha's look. 'Yes, Andreas is going. Apparently the choir walks up the hill with lighted candles, singing all the way.'

The fireworks started as soon as it got dark. They could hear the merriment in the village from their villa as they got ready, with the windows wide open so they could watch for the rockets. The cat, although used to it, decided that under the bed was a good place to be. Sasha stroked him and soothed him before they left the villa, and left him a piece of fresh fish. Then she scrubbed the smell of fish from her hands, and picked some lavender, crushing it between her palms to bring out the beauty of the scent.

The entire village was dancing. Coloured lights were strung up round the houses and shops, and even the fishing-boats were lit up. The harbour and jetty were packed with people, all laughing and singing and dancing to pipers and mandolins and fiddlers. There was no need of a partner—strangers danced with strangers, whole rows of people linking arms and losing themselves in the spirit of the dance. Every time Sasha thought she recognised Andreas, or Artemis, or the landlord of the taverna, they would be lost in the crush, so she contented herself with dancing and losing her inhibitions to the heady rhythms all around her. Barbie had long been swallowed up. But it didn't matter, because as midnight approached the crowds became quieter, and with the candle-lit procession of choirboys and men the villagers fell silent, and followed the twinkling lights up the hill, along the path that wound round the olive groves to the church with its gold-painted spire.

The service was simple, half in Greek and half in English. Sasha spotted Barbie's light head next to Andreas's dark one in the flickering candlelight, but she didn't bother to sit by them. She was content to watch and take part in the timeless ritual of celebrating the birth of a Child. The solo choirboy sang like an angel, and Sasha had tears in her eyes as she left the church and the crowd began their downhill stroll, quieter now, but still greeting each other and singing a little in groups. It was Christmas Day, and such a Christmas she had never experienced. It was something she wanted to remember, to take home with her as one of her loveliest memories, so she lagged behind the rest, allowing others to overtake her on the steep path.

Then someone behind her said gently, 'You enjoyed the service?'

She couldn't mistake the voice; it was ingrained in her heart. She turned round slowly. 'Adam! It's really you!' They stood staring at each other while a tumult of rejoicing went on inside her. Then, as he took both her hands in his, she whispered, 'Merry Christmas.'

'Merry Christmas, Sasha.' He leaned towards her and their cheeks touched as he kissed her gently. The little island, which had been magic enough before, suddenly exploded and electrified and burst into flames of joy. It was already one of the most beautiful evenings of her life. Now she knew that nothing could ever match the happiness that flooded into her heart at that moment. She knew that she had been longing for him secretly, trying not to allow her thoughts to go back to the grey eyes and the gentle voice she loved so very much.

It seemed hard to have to translate her bursting joy into mundane speech, but she managed it. 'How did you manage to get away?'

'I managed it. Got a cancellation.'

'That was lucky.'

'Yes. How is Barbie?'

'She's feeling wonderful, thanks to you. How are you, Adam?'

'Fine, thanks.' They tagged along behind the rest of the village, Sasha drinking in every detail of the little scene as they congregated in groups around the dark waters of the still harbour that reflected the lights from the eaves of the houses. He was wearing a shirt open at the neck, and light-coloured trousers, and his hair was boyishly curled round his face, instead of sleeked back as it usually was in the wards. He put his arm gently round her shoulders. 'You like the villa, then?'

'Everything is just wonderful.'

'I hope——' But he was interrupted by a noisy group who had been laughing outside the taverna. Sasha saw that Andreas and Barbie were in the middle, but she didn't know the others—at first. Adam said, 'Why, it's Alex!' and he strode over to shake a distinguished white-haired man by the hand. He was lost for a moment in hugs and greetings, before turning back to Sasha. 'Let me introduce Sasha.' The white-haired man was the father of Andreas, and owner of the *Dolphin*. With him were his personal servant and his secretary. And behind them was a jet-haired beauty dressed in crimson and gold, whom Adam took in his arms and kissed soundly. 'This is Artemis, Sasha. You saw her photograph.'

Artemis kissed Sasha's cheek and wished her a happy Christmas. But she at once linked arms with Adam, and told him he was naughty for not letting them know he was coming.

Sasha found herself alone for a moment. Then the fair-haired secretary came and took her arm. 'I'm John Steadman. Alex didn't introduce me, because I'm an employee, but I don't take offence—that's just my peasant master showing his colours.' His voice was perfect public-school English. 'He needs me every step of the way—to show him how real gentlemen behave!' He was attractive, young, with piercing blue eyes. But the eyes held cold steel and, in spite of his good looks, Sasha wasn't impressed. He said, 'I'm glad you're coming to the party, Sasha. Apart from Artemis—who's a bit old for me—there's not a single decent bird in view.'

Sasha hadn't come through five years at Liverpool University without a little smattering of how to treat unwelcome advances. She was just trying to think up

one of her best withering replies when, from the corner
of her eye, she saw Artemis and Adam with their arms
around each other's waist, talking together at the back
of the group. And the pain was bad. She smiled at John
Steadman. 'Well, we wouldn't want the party to get too
geriatric,' she said, making her voice warm.

'I say, maybe I could walk you home?' John said,
moving visibly closer.

Alex Daniacos called across the group, 'Sasha, watch
out for that guy! He isn't called the Don Juan of the
Dolphin for nothing.'

Sasha kept up the pretence. 'We young ones must
stick together,' she called back, and laughed up at John
Steadman, who put her hand in the crook of his arm
with a self-satisfied smile.

'I'm just seeing Sasha home.'

Adam's cool, polite voice had a way of cutting
through the general conversation, and it did so now.
'No need, John, thank you. I'll see the girls back, as
we're all staying in my villa.'

'Oh, not yet, Adam, please?' Barbie was clearly not
ready for bed.

Sasha said, 'We'd better get some rest.'

John agreed quickly. 'You'll need all your stamina
for one of Alex's parties. I'll pick you all up in the boat
at three.'

And Andreas interrupted to say, 'Unless I get there
first.' It seemed that the Daniacos family had trouble
keeping their rather cocky secretary in his place. He
took Barbie out of hearing to say goodnight. Sasha
quickly said goodnight to Alex and John. When she
turned to Artemis, she had her arms locked around
Adam's neck and they were kissing. She felt as though
she had been kicked in the stomach.

It was Barbie who went to her, saw where she was
looking. 'I knew you liked him, Sasha,' she said quietly,
'but I didn't realise how much.'

Sasha turned away to look over the harbour. 'It
doesn't show, does it?'

'Not now. You look OK now. Adam's coming—better smile or something!' And both girls turned to meet Adam, who had just waved to Alex, and now strode across to join them, his hair untidy and brightness in his eyes. It was quite clear why he had made the time to come to Zaramos for Christmas. As the three of them walked back along the shadowy coastal road they could see the party from the yacht making their way back in small speedboats. The lights from the *Dolphin* were reflected in the still waters of the bay, and it was visible all the way round until they got to Adam's villa.

Barbie made conversation, as Sasha was silent. 'Adam, you seem very much at home here. Why do you bother going back to Liverpool?'

Sasha frowned at her, but Adam didn't seem to think the question any way impertinent. 'I love the place—but, let's face it, how would I earn my keep? Not much neurosurgery on Zaramos.'

Barbie went on, 'There might be if Alex gets his way and builds a huge holiday complex.'

'That's a long way away. Some of the locals are protesting about it, while the other half are longing for the extra money it will bring the village. I think I'll stay on the sidelines in this contest.' He sighed with pleasure as the villa came into view. 'It's always good to come back.'

Sasha spoke for the first time, feeling suddenly slightly guilty about the state of the bathroom. 'I'm afraid it isn't very tidy.'

Adam looked at her with a quiet smile. 'I'd be furious with you if it were. You two are here to enjoy yourselves, not act as housekeepers.'

'We're doing that, Adam.' Barbie ran in and opened the front door, while Sasha paused to stroke Emperor at the gate by the lavender bush. 'This is the best and happiest holiday of my life.'

'Good. It was meant to be. And tomorrow should be fun, too.'

Barbie said, 'I'm going to bed this very minute, so

that I'll be in good shape for an all-day party. Goodnight.' And she ran to the bathroom. Adam looked around his long, comfortable living-room, and went to the drinks cabinet, coming back with a bottle of ouzo and two glasses.

'A Christmas drink?' He handed one to Sasha. It seemed suddenly very quiet after the boisterous fun of the evening. They sat down, not very close together, and the little clock struck two. Sasha leaned her head back, suddenly tired—not physically so much, but weary in her heart. She reached out and put on the small table-lamp. 'You're quiet, Sasha.'

'It's nice to see you,' she said. 'How long have you got?'

'Two days.' He smiled.

'You came all this way for two days?'

'Yes—and do you know why?' His eyes were twinkling, though his face was still grave.

She hesitated before replying, looked down at the sweet, sticky liquid in her glass, noting the way it stuck to the sides as she twirled it. 'It's fairly obvious, if you don't mind my saying so.' He did smile then, and she went on quickly, getting it over, 'I'm glad, really. You were always so lonely—no, not lonely—you were self-contained, but always alone, if you know what I mean. I'm glad—really glad—that you have a good friend here—it must be precious to you.'

Something crossed his face then, a brief show of vulnerability, of naked need. He cleared his throat, but said nothing. Then he stood up and drew her to her feet. 'You're so lovely. Happy Christmas, my darling.' And he kissed her gently but firmly, holding her close until her own arms encircled his warm, hard body, and for a few sweet moments they stood as one in the still, scented night.

The sound of the bathroom lock being opened made him draw back. Sasha felt close to tears. He ought not to have done that—it only reminded her how much she wanted him. 'My turn,' she mumbled. 'Goodnight.' She

washed hastily and brushed her teeth, walking quickly into the bedroom without looking back at the living-room, where the light was still lit. She scrambled into bed. ''Night, Barbie.' But Barbie was asleep, and Sasha lay awake for another hour, listening to Adam as on catlike feet he wandered around his Zaramos home for a while before turning in.

It was late when she slept, but very late when she woke. The sun was streaming in, and Adam Harrington stood there in shorts and T-shirt, holding a tray with two mugs of tea. 'I couldn't remember if you took sugar, so the basin is on the tray.' He smiled and set it down. 'I'll be in the sea, if either of you feels like a race.' He left them to get ready. Barbie refused to swim, preferring to laze on the patio with a plate of cornflakes and a pot of coffee, with Emperor on her knee. Sasha put on her bikini, and a shirt over it. There was a slight breeze, but it was warm enough to swim, and she knew the exercise would help her to unwind mentally. She plunged into the water, gasping at first, as it was cooler than it looked. Then she set off to swim out to the rock where Adam was waving, looking slim and handsome as he hung on, waiting for her.

'I'll let you rest before we race back. It's quite a long way, and I probably get more practice.'

'That's very noble of you, but I daresay you'll win anyway.' She pulled herself up and sat by him—not close enough that their skin touched, but enough to want it to.

'Next time you come you'll be more used to the water.' So he meant to invite them again. It was a kind thought, but did she want to see him so close with Artemis? The pain would still be there, she knew, when she saw them together.

'Give me a start,' she said, suddenly launching herself into the race back to the shore. She struck out strongly, knowing herself to be a reasonable swimmer, even without too much practice. They were almost on the beach when he caught up with her, finally overtaking with a few feet to spare.

He hauled her back into deeper water. 'You deserve
to be ducked for cheating like that!' And he pulled her
under, where she turned a complete somersault to
escape from him. When he caught up with her again his
arms trapped her firmly, and she closed her eyes,
screwing them up ready for the splash. Instead she felt
his salty lips on hers, and their bodies moulded together
in the water. The sensation of closeness overwhelmed
her, and she clung to him until they both sank under the
clear water, when they parted and surfaced. She started
to swim to the shore, but he caught her again, and
carried her, protesting, high up on the beach, before he
allowed her to slip against his body to the ground.

Barbie was waiting as they ran up to the villa
together. She saw from Sasha's face that the situation
was tense again, and she said cheerfully, 'Adam, you'll
have to advise me—what do people eat for lunch when
they are going to dine on a millionaire's yacht?'

'Not too much,' he grinned. 'Fruit—there are fresh
figs and melons—and a slice of cheese should be
enough. Hospitality is something the Daniacos family is
very good at.' He smoothed back his hair, his arm
dripping and his body shiny wet, and Sasha felt she had
never seen a man so beautiful before. 'I think I'll
shower before you two—I understand women need a
long time to get ready!'

Sasha wrapped the shirt around her. She smiled at
Barbie's look of curiosity. 'He swims well,' she
volunteered.

Barbie looked knowing. 'I was watching,' she said
with a wink, as she made her way to the kitchen. 'No, I
don't need any help to wash a few figs and slice a couple
of melons. You go and decide what to wear.'

At three they all emerged from their rooms, and
Adam was appreciative of their efforts. 'What a
difference from those urchins I met this morning.
Sasha, why haven't I seen you in that dress before?' She
was wearing her blue chiffon, which flattered her waist

and sun-kissed arms.

Barbie said, 'That's simple—because you've never invited her to dine on a yacht before.'

Adam smiled. 'Then we shall have to do it more often.'

They walked down to the beach in the warm sunshine. Barbie said, 'I'll just never forget this Christmas as long as I live.' And she ran down to the water's edge, where she could see more clearly that someone was just coming down the ladder to the small boat bobbing beside the *Dolphin*.

Adam said, 'I saw Joe before I came.'

There was something in his voice—she looked up at him. 'Adam, how is he? Last time we saw him, I thought he was much better. The anger had gone from his voice.'

'I think he needs investigating. The anger has gone, I noticed—but so has all feeling and all emotion. His eyes are blank. You must get him to see Slade—unless you send him to me. I'll see him privately—if he'll come. There just might be a CNS lesion, and if so, the sooner he's persuaded to come, the better.'

'Something in his brain? Oh, poor Joe—I never suspected that. But he has always refused when I asked him, Adam—and I've got my exams coming up almost as soon as we get back.'

The motor-boat was almost there, driven by a smiling Andreas. Adam said, 'We'll talk again. I'm sure it will do after your exams. I know how keyed up you must be. Get the Primary over, and then we'll see to Joe.'

'If you're sure.'

'It may be nothing—just my suspicious mind. Anyway, we can do nothing now, so let's get on board and just enjoy the party.'

Andreas let out a blast on his hooter, and swung round so that a wall of fine spray splashed Barbie's dress as she stood close to the edge. She shook her fist at Andreas as he sprang ashore, wearing a shirt and bow-tie over a pair of shorts. It was soon clear why, as he splashed in the shallows to carry the girls to the boat.

Adam rolled up his trousers and climbed in, his shiny black evening shoes in his hand.

The champagne was flowing almost as soon as they arrived on board. Fairy lights were lit, and when the sun began to set the lights sparkled against a silken sky, luminously lovely. John Steadman came to greet them, in a perfectly fitting white dinner-jacket. 'Now that Adam has brought his harem, the music can begin.' He took Sasha's hand and kissed it. 'You look divine. I give you warning that you are about to be monopolised.'

Sasha smiled, but her mind was concentrating on looking for Artemis. There was no sign of her yet, and Adam stood chatting to Andreas and Barbie. John turned up the volume of the expensive sound system. 'Dance with me, Sasha.' She put her champagne glass down and allowed herself to be held in a close embrace, John's well-shaved cheek, smelling of expensive aftershave close against hers, smelling of lavender. She didn't care tuppence for the young Englishman, but it was delightful to dance in the twilight to the lilting Greek rhythms, to be part—just for once—of the life of the really wealthy.

They had danced for quite a long time when someone tapped John's shoulder and prised them apart. 'Do you mind, John?' It was Adam.

John looked annoyed. 'If you must!'

Adam took Sasha in his arms, and she felt light and comfortable in his embrace, as though she could dance forever. He whispered, 'I thought you might need rescuing. John is a bit of an anaconda with women.'

Sasha said rather sourly, 'You mean Artemis isn't ready yet? I was quite enjoying myself.'

Adam said nothing, but she felt his body tense. He held her close, and they danced close, but not cheek to cheek. As always when she was near him, she relaxed and moved imperceptibly closer to his length, and they moved as one person in the starlit night. Nothing more was spoken as they danced further away from the others, until they were at the bow of the yacht, alone.

Then he kissed her, and her feet no longer danced as time stood still, and they were in their own world, with only the gentle lapping of the water against the hull, and the distant call of a seabird.

And then suddenly he was being pulled away from her, and John was saying, 'Come, come, Adam, you can't have her all to yourself, you know. The party's starting, and I've come to collect my nightbird.' He drew Sasha into his arms. But Adam snatched her at once away from John. She was vaguely aware there were more people on the deck than before. But there was no time to check before Adam's fist shot out, cracked with a thud against John Steadman's chin, and sent him sprawling to the deck.

One of the women screamed, and voices jumbled as members of the crew ran to pick John up. But he waved them away, scrambling to his feet and saying in a voice of forced cheerfulness, 'Nothing's broken, fortunately for some.' He brushed down his jacket, looking under his eyebrows at Adam, who was rubbing his knuckles as though he didn't quite realise what he had done. John stood facing them, looking from one to the other. Then he said with a mocking smile, 'So our man of ice has finally melted, eh?'

Adam said, his lips taut, 'I shouldn't have done it. I'm sorry.'

'No hard feelings.' John was getting his cocky manner back. 'But you won't mind if I have a dance with the lady—just to make up?' And he deliberately put his arm round Sasha and led her away. 'I think we both need a drink,' he whispered, as the general chat started again all round them.

From the corner of her eye, Sasha saw Adam move to the railing alone, and lean there, looking out. She knew John was chatting, but she didn't listen, her heart yearning for that lonely man whose civilised exterior had just been breached. She tried to tell herself that his kisses meant nothing, that she treated them as he did, as a trifling diversion. But it was hard to convince herself.

But then a svelte figure in a silver sheath swayed elegantly towards him, and his face was hidden by a cascade of raven hair. Artemis was here, and, from the look of it, worth waiting for. She was already dancing with Adam. John Steadman was saying, 'You must come and take a look at the ship. I recommend my cabin!' And Sasha nodded, unaware of what he had said.

CHAPTER SEVEN

WITH his arm securely round Sasha's waist—'in case the ship rolls unexpectedly'—John Steadman took her down the main companion-way, past the luxurious lounge cabin, where a table was set with shining crystal and silver. He briefly explained each part of the yacht, but she noticed with amusement that he was steering her very definitely towards the living quarters and his own cabin. 'I took this job on temporarily, as a way of seeing the world after Cambridge—but I became addicted. I've been with Alex for five years now, and I'm always telling myself that I ought to be in the Stock Exchange with my father, making my own millions.'

'And do tell me—what did Alex mean when he called you a Don Juan?' She was teasing him, but so mildly that he didn't notice. 'And someone else warned me that you could be a bit of an anaconda. I wonder why?'

John seemed flattered by the reputation. 'I'm a normal young man,' he grinned. 'Perhaps this is what they meant.' And he swiftly caught her in a tight embrace, from which she could not escape. Nor could she push him away, as he had pinioned her arms so skilfully. He then proceeded to kiss her with a great deal of force and very little skill, so that she emerged gasping for breath, feeling as though she had been attacked by a sink plunger. He said, 'I can see you're lost in admiration. Let me show you my cabin—I arranged the décor myself, and it's a bit more tasteful than old Alex's—he's all for ostentation everywhere.'

Sasha was fortunately saved from having to run away by the timely appearance of Alex Daniacos himself, resplendent in evening dress, with diamonds on the front of his shirt, in his rings and smothering the face of his

101

watch. 'I heard that, young John.' He didn't seem perturbed by his secretary's sneers. 'Sasha, you are looking beautiful. Please allow me to escort you to the main deck. This is no time for playing hide-and-seek, John!' As Sasha took Alex's arm he winked at her, and she felt a new kind of affection for Adam's old friend. John could only follow tamely behind, like a defeated gladiator. As they appeared on deck Alex was given a burst of applause. He acknowledged it with a modest wave, and set out to greet each of his guests personally.

'Sasha, this is Dmitri, my architect. He and I are going to be rich when our holiday village is built.' Sasha shook hands with the small dark man, noticing that he had been chatting with Adam and Artemis as they came up. 'Dmitri, after dinner Sasha must see our plans.' He moved off, leaving Sasha speaking to the architect. Very soon John Steadman managed to get her to dance again, and she made no protest—he had done nothing to frighten her off, in spite of Adam's warning. She wondered if by any chance Adam might be a tiny bit jealous of the younger man. Yet how could he, when he had the devoted attention of one of the loveliest women in Greece?

The meal was served on silver plates by a team of waiters, with background music played by a group of talented men who switched from guitars to bouzoukis at a snap of Alex's fingers. Sasha remembered Adam's comment that the Daniacos hospitality was lavish, and sensibly ate sparingly as course followed course of fascinating food, finishing with crêpes Suzette flamed to perfection. The champagne was served throughout the meal until the sweets and coffee were brought, when dozens of liqueurs were wheeled in on a silver filigree trolley.

John proved a good conversationalist, and they chatted about the places the yacht visited, in between speeches by Alex, whose voice was loud, and who was enjoying himself with verbal sparring with his son Andreas, who did not approve of the plans to alter the character of Zaramos village. When they demanded that Adam take sides, he said, 'I am impartial. But I warn you, old friend, that if you put that monstrosity on Zaramos hillside, I won't be returning.' He was laughing, but it was clear he supported his colleague Andreas.

Alex seemed unperturbed. 'You will see, Adam—it will be magnificent, yes, Dmitri? It will win awards for its beauty, fame for its creators, and it will attract money to the island, to make roads and sewers. You will see in the near future who is right. I have lived in poverty, so I know how these people feel about it. They will love to have modern comforts. You are all spoiled rich people, who have no knowledge of how the poor have to live.'

Adam reached across the table and shook his hand. 'You may be right. Shall we give it a year? I'll come back next Christmas, and we'll see then how good your judgement of people is?'

Dmitri joked, 'His judgement of money hasn't let him down yet.' Later they took their glasses on deck. The musicians played slow, sweet music, and some couples danced. Barbie was enfolded in Andreas's arms, a look of total contentment on her face.

After dancing with Alex, Sasha said, 'I'd like to go back, if it doesn't offend you. I'm very tired.' In fact, she had seen John edging his way closer, and decided that she was too tired to keep on avoiding his obvious intentions.

'I understand.' He smiled and beckoned to one of the waiters. 'I'll get one of my sailors to take you ashore——'

Adam Harrington's quiet voice cut into their conversation. 'No need for that, Alex. I'll take one of your boats and leave it at the jetty. I must be up early to get back for my plane. I'm operating tomorrow.'

He must have already said his goodbyes to Artemis, who was not to be seen. Alex shook his hand warmly, and embraced him. 'I hope we see you before a year is out.' They climbed down to one of the small boats, which Adam had clearly handled before. Alex and Andreas waved from the yacht. Barbie clearly intended to dance until the musicians grew weary.

'I hope you didn't leave because of me, Adam.' The boat swished through the water towards the harbour, and the yacht looked inviting, with its coloured lights and music, and elegant people on deck.

'Not at all. I do need my sleep. I really am operating tomorrow when I get back, and it would be foolish to stay.' He steered skilfully into the jetty, close by the harbour wall, and tied the boat up at a mooring. Then he quickly jumped out and gave Sasha a hand as she manipulated the folds of her chiffon dress on to the wooden jetty. They turned to walk the few yards round the headland to the villa, with the sea lapping on the rocks and the sound of the crickets shrilling in the grass at the side of the winding road. 'So what do you think of the Daniacos family?' he asked.

'It was all quite fascinating. Wonderful. The secretary was a bit much, though.'

'He is rather pushy. He isn't used to being turned down—most women fall into his arms.'

'He isn't used to being knocked down, either, from what I could see.'

Adam said shortly, 'He asked for it.'

They reached the villa and were greeted by Emperor. 'Nightcap?' asked Adam.

'Yes, please.' Sasha sat on the sofa and Emperor curled up on her knee. She knew that once they got back to Liverpool Adam would become the distant senior consultant. She wanted tonight to go on for a while, where they could both pretend that they could be friends. As he handed her the glass, she said, 'This time last year I only knew you by sight—and by reputation, of course.'

Adam sat down next to her, and their thighs touched naturally, as though it was usual for them to sit so close. 'I knew you by sight, too. I recall asking Pat Moore who the dark, slim houseman was.'

'Did you really notice me?'

'Oh, yes. And I remember what he said. He told me you were very reserved, and looked like one of those bookish types who wouldn't be any fun to take out.'

Sasha laughed and put her glass on the table so as not to spill it over the cat on her knee. 'He's quite right, of course. Even tonight I've made you leave the party.'

'Not made me. I felt the same—too much of a good thing, staying till the very end. Besides, we both need some sleep.'

'Yes. Do you remember how you felt when you took your Primary exam?'

'I'm not so old that I can't think back so far.' He smiled and put one arm along the back of the sofa behind her. It was only natural that they leaned closer together, that his hand began to play with a strand of her hair as they talked of times past, of their student days, and the things they already shared in their work, and their likes and dislikes. She could have listened to his gentle, comfortable voice forever. He got up to refill their glasses, but as soon as he sat down again she nestled into the crook of his arm, feeling totally content just to listen to him, to make the most of this last time together.

She asked him about Joe. 'I'll ring him at work—try to get him to pop along to the department for a check-up.'

'Thanks, Adam. I seem to be thanking you all the time.'

'It's nothing. What we're here for, after all.' And he stroked the cat on her knee before putting his arm back loosely round her shoulders, which definitely seemed the best place for it to be. She realised that they were closer than they had ever been during their passionate embraces, that this quiet evening together had cemented them forever as friends as well as being physically attracted to each other. She felt richly satisfied as the hours passed, and neither of them seemed tired, finding more and more things to say to each other, things that made them understand about each other's past life. Adam spoke about Deborah more freely, about the early problems of marrying another doctor, how their time off never seemed to coincide. It seemed to Sasha that the sadness was no longer in his eyes when he spoke of his wife, that he had consigned her at last to his past.

Perhaps Artemis Daniacos had helped—perhaps this time he had decided to ask her to be his wife?

The buzzing sound of a motor-boat intruded on their conversation. Adam looked at the clock. 'It's almost morning! I say, I'd better turn in. I don't want Andreas feeling hurt because we left the party early. Goodnight, my dear. I'll be off before you wake.' He was behind the sofa now, as Emperor opened one eye, knowing that he would soon have to find another cosy resting-place. Adam leaned down and kissed Sasha gently on the cheek. It was a slow, real kiss, not a hurried peck. After he had gone to bed, Sasha sat with her fingers to the spot, trying not to be sad because it was the last.

Adam was gone when the girls finally rose next morning. Sasha had been up first, wandering round the villa, plumping up cushions and washing the cups and glasses they had left in the sink from the previous wonderful, momentous day. It was like a dream, the party and the yacht, the jewels and the silver and the throbbing, haunting music . . . And now they had three more days before they themselves packed their bags.

And then, as the villa was tidy and Barbie still totally unconscious in bed, Sasha decided that mooching around wouldn't help her feeling of depression, that she would be better taking a brisk walk in the sun. She was just brushing her hair and trying to insert her feet into her sandals without bending down, when there was a gentle tap on the door. Curious, she went to answer it. John Steadman stood there, with a beautiful bouquet. 'For you, Princess.'

'Thank you, John! They're beautiful—and so fragrant.'

'So are you.' He said it as though he meant it. She had no choice but to invite him in. She put the flowers in a vase, and some coffee in the filter. She felt rather under-dressed in her cotton jeans and shirt, but John was complimentary. 'You're different, Sasha.'

'I know what I am—I've been told. I'm bookish and not much fun.' She smiled as she recalled Pat Moore's assessment of her.

'That can be altered. Sasha—you've only three more

days. Why don't you come to Kourikes for the day tomorrow? You two with me and Andreas? It would be fun to go as a four, wouldn't it?'

'I suppose it would. Barbie's still asleep——'

'Oh, no, I'm not.' Barbie came in, fully dressed. 'It's a terrific idea, and I've already told Andreas we're going.'

John smiled. 'Right. We'll pick you up in the fast boat tomorrow morning.' He gave them a wave, and left them.

Sasha turned to her friend. 'That's all very well, Barb, but you're not to leave me alone with that—that anaconda!'

'I promise. But you've no need to worry. Just remember your karate lessons Joe gave you.'

'Dear old Joe.' Sasha thought back to her one-time best friend. Then she laughed. 'I can hardly see myself throwing John Steadman over my shoulder—he's much too refined!'

Barbie drank her coffee. 'Life is flat. What shall we do today?'

'We should go right to the top of the hill past the church, for a last look at our magic island.' And for once Barbie agreed to walk. They took their time, walking up through the woods, not particularly keeping to the paths, except where the land was fenced off by private farms and villas. Black goats grazed at will. Peasants in black clothes tended their goats, or took their chickens and fruits to sell in the village, loaded on gentle mules. Sasha and Barbie sat for a while on top of the hill until the wind got up and they felt chilled.

'I'll never forget this island. Or Adam,' said Barbara. 'Even though I'm a nobody, Adam thought I was worth being nice to. It's really marvellous when you meet people like him.'

'You're a doctor, aren't you? You've worked hard to be one. People in medicine do respect one another. After all, in our own way, we spend our lives helping people who happen to be less fortunate than we are. See what I mean?'

'I think so.' She looked sideways at her friend as they tramped down the hill. 'I won't miss Andreas—but I'll think of him sometimes. At least you've still got Adam.'

'I'll see him in passing, of course. But you've seen

Artemis. Can you see now why he hasn't settled down with a nice local girl? It's obvious to me.' Sasha was being down-to-earth and sensible.

'Did he kiss you last night?'

The question was too sudden to lie about. 'Yes, once.' Barbie shrugged. 'Oh, well, that's life.'

'You've got Kourikes to look forward to.'

'Sure.' And as they walked steadily downhill, looking forward to a glass of wine when they reached the village, Sasha hugged to herself the memory of last night, when they talked the night away and hardly noticed the time.

The trip to the neighbouring island next day was fun, particularly for Barbie, who was with Andreas. Sasha was wary, hoping that John would not live up to his reputation. But she couldn't help enjoying the boat trip, which was very fast. As her heart leapt at the way the wind came at them and took their breath away, she was glad John was there to hold on to. They landed in a quiet cove, where lunch at a small family restaurant was delicious. 'Grateful patients of mine,' explained Andreas, as they thanked the owner. 'They thought he was dying—but, poor man, all he had was diabetes. Right as rain now.'

'I suggest a guided tour of the caves now,' said John.

'What caves?'

'Would you believe the caves where the Minotaur lived? Where the famous labyrinth was?'

Barbie and Sasha both shook their heads. Andreas said, 'Ah, but did you know that there was more than one Minotaur? After all, the little islands have their living to earn too, you know!' So, with a sense of the ridiculous, they joined the groups of tourists who were being shown round the carefully stage-managed caverns among the black rocks. Sasha realised why they had come down as soon as they lost sight of Andreas and Barbie. There were lots of small side caves, where people could wander freely. But although John put his arm round her waist, and kissed her two or three times as they wandered, he definitely behaved in a most gentlemanly manner, for which she was very relieved.

That night, from her bed, in the shadowy lavender-smelling night, Barbie whispered, 'It was a nice day. A nice fortnight.'

'Perfect,' Sasha whispered back.

'I'm glad Adam came too. After all, it is his villa.'

'He only came to see Artemis.'

'I think he's fond of you, too.'

'I doubt it.'

'I wonder what the weather's like in Liverpool?'

'Lousy, I expect.'

They were right. It was raining when they arrived back in the residence and humped their cases up the chilly stairs to their flats. Sasha dumped her suitcase, splashed her hands and face, and then went straight to the phone and rang Joe. While the phone rang she could hear the sound of raindrops on the window, and the dismal groan of car engines as they changed gear at the corner of the road. Then an unknown voice said 'Hello?'

'It's Sasha Norton here. May I speak to Joe?'

'Oh, Dr Norton, it's Joe's mate Terry. I thought you knew. He's gone into hospital this morning. Mr Harrington's ward.'

'Oh, no!'

'He's had some tests. I've been to see him tonight. Seems cheerful enough.'

'Do you think I'd be allowed to visit, Terry?'

'You being a doctor, I can't see as they'd mind.'

She changed into warm clothes, and went across at once to Neuro. The sister was someone she hadn't met before, but she confirmed that Joe had been admitted with a possible tumour. 'Oh, poor Joe.'

Sister's eyes were kind. 'He's not in pain, Doctor. Just a bit blank when you talk to him. As if he's in a dream—can't connect his sentences, and forgets what he wants to say.' She led the way to a small single room. 'Don't stay long. He's tired after all the tests, and he's having his angiograms tomorrow.'

'What drugs is he on?'

'Anticonvulsants and steroids at the moment.'

'I see. Thank you, Sister.' Sasha opened the door and

went in. Joe lay, fast asleep. She stood for a moment, then bent and kissed his cheek. 'I'll be here, Joe. I won't let you down,' she whispered. He looked so peaceful and strong, his healthy muscles showing through the pyjamas, with no sign of flab or fat on him. 'How could anyone looking so fit have something wrong?'

Sister said quietly, 'It will help him get over the surgery, him being such a fit man.'

Sasha sat for a moment by the sleeping figure. Already the room was filled with get-well cards from his staff and his friends. Lights were being put off along the corridor, and she stood up to go. 'God bless you, my Joe,' she whispered as she closed the door to. She walked slowly along the corridor, dimly lit now, her shoes making no noise in the hushed, empty atmosphere. If only she had made Joe go to the doctors earlier. Now he was on anticonvulsants, and the speed of his admission indicated that his condition was serious. Sasha had been closest to him, had seen the change in him. Why, oh, why had she not done more about it?

She waited for the lift, heard it swishing up the shaft from the ground floor. The doors hissed and opened—and Adam Harrington stepped out, dressed in his grey suit, his hair sleeked back showing the grey over his ears . . . His eyes showed concern. 'You've seen him?' The lift doors hissed and closed behind him, but neither of them noticed.

She nodded. 'He's sleeping.'

He took a folder from under his arm. 'Come and take a look at the tomograph.' She followed him into his office, where he put on the light and woke the sleeping room by moving chairs and rearranging the desk. He took out some films. It was blatantly obvious that one side of Joe's brain was being pushed to the side by some large soft-tissue lesion.

She looked at Adam with dull eyes. 'Meningioma?'

He nodded. 'Without doubt. Anything else that size and he'd be dead by now.'

She swallowed and tried to keep her composure. 'You—can do it? The operation? You can remove the tumour?

'It may not be easy. I'll wait until the angiogram before I can say for sure. Poor chap—he could have been carrying that around with him for years.'

'It's a wonder he could do his job.' Sasha felt helpless. 'I was the one who recognised his change of personality—a good twelve months ago, now that I think back. It's my fault completely. I should have insisted on him seeing someone a long time ago. If he dies——'

Adam said quickly, 'Wait till we do all the tests. No point in getting emotional.'

'It's all right for you——' Sasha stopped herself. 'I'm sorry.' They faced each other across Adam's desk, the photograph of Joe's tumour between them. It seemed symbolic—Joe's illness had brought Sasha back to him. Her loyalty and her guilt feelings would see to that. She faced Adam and couldn't think of anything to say. 'I'm sorry,' she repeated.

Adam said quietly, 'You mustn't go back to him if you aren't in love with him.'

'That's not important. He needs me.'

'You can't live a lie.'

'There's nothing else to do.'

'But there has to be!' Adam took a deep breath, gripped the edge of the table with both hands. 'Look, Sasha, you're tired. We'll talk again. Come up about five tomorrow—I'll have the angiogram by then.'

'Thank you.' She turned and went to the door, which he opened for her. She passed so close to him that memories of that last night on Zaramos flooded about her so strongly that she almost turned and pleaded for his embrace, his touch—anything to comfort her. But she carried on, unable to think of anything that could keep her with him any longer. She felt very alone as she walked back across the car park in the bleak and cold of a late December night. Her tears mingled with the rain on her cheeks as she remembered the great happiness that now seemed centuries away.

Suddenly a dark figure emerged from the shadows of

the building and threw himself at her in a rugby tackle,
bringing her to the ground and smothering her mouth
with a gloved hand before she had time to scream. He
dragged her coat open and viciously pulled up her skirt,
forcing her legs apart with his other hand. She heard a
hoarse whisper, 'I've gorra knife!' Gasping for breath,
she thought back to the lessons in self-defence she had
been taught. She ought to have been alert enough to stop
him getting her to the ground. But now she was here she
tried to remember Joe's words, as he'd jollied the girls
along into practising defending themselves.

'Go for the eyes or the goolies—and fast!' Joe had
said. It was something that they had never been able to
take seriously when practising in a comfortable, warm
gym. But now she was straddled on the cold, wet ground,
and the man grappling with her was stronger and very
determined. Sasha freed one arm and, while she went for
his eyes, gleaming through the slit in the balaclava, she
brought one knee up as hard as she could into his groin.
He shrieked and rolled over momentarily, and in that
moment she was able to scream. She had never screamed
before, but she screamed, took a breath, and then went
on screaming. People came running. She saw the man
dragged up and hustled away by security men. She heard
the wail of a siren, and knew the police were here. Before
he was hauled out of the beam of the security man's
torch, Sasha caught a glimpse of the face as his balaclava
was torn off. He was white, with pale, shifty eyes and a
stubble of beard. She had never seen him before in her
life.

'Doctor, would you like to come along to Casualty?'

'Are you all right, Sasha?'

'Better come along and let Dr Mortimer take a look at
you.' She was surrounded by helping hands. But there
was only one figure she needed—and as she looked
around the pale circle of faces she recognised it, and went
wordlessly into Adam's hard embrace.

'She's all right. Dr Green and I will get her to her
room.'

Still held very tightly, she looked up at Adam. 'I must look a mess.'

'Thank heaven you're safe.'

'It wasn't Joe.' She was sobbing now. 'It wasn't Joe.'

His grip tightened. 'I'll see you home. You're a very brave girl.'

'I only did what Joe taught me.'

Barbie came and took her arm. 'Here, let me help. What you need is a hot bath and a cup of tea.' They went in, and Adam's grip seemed to lessen. As Sasha took control of her own walking, she looked round, only to see him walking away, his outline blurred by the driving rain. Barbie said quietly, 'Don't look back, love—you'll only upset yourself. He's doing the right thing, you know.'

Sasha was grateful for the tea, and for the hot bath Barbie ran for her. A policewoman came and took some evidence in a comforting voice, and then she went to bed. Barbie waited until she was calm before she left her.

It was then that Sasha cried properly—cried bitter tears because Adam couldn't be there any more, and they both knew it. Joe was in the clear. Gary Brooks was in the clear. That gave her strength. She would call on Bella and give her the good news herself. She slept at last—yet in her sleep she wrapped her arms about herself as though she was still holding on to Adam Harrington in the bows of the yacht *Dolphin*. When she woke to the pale sunshine of a December morning the tears were still wet on her eyelashes.

It would have been easy to feel sorry for herself, to stay in bed and allow her friends and colleagues to make a fuss of her. But she hadn't been hurt, only frightened for a moment or two. And Joe needed her. So did Gary Brooks—who thought he was still under suspicion of this crime. She made a strong cup of coffee and forced herself to eat a bowl of muesli, though that day it tasted of sawdust. Then she went out into a surprisingly bright morning, the frost melting and the condensation dripping from the windows in the flat and in the bus she took to

Gary Brooks' home.

Bella Brooks didn't recognise her at first, with her scarf pulled up to keep her nose warm. She drew it down. 'I thought you'd like to know they've caught the "Western Prowler", Mrs Brooks.'

'Come in, come in, Doctor. You look ill, love.'

'It was me he attacked.'

Bella Brooks was touched. 'Oh, my, you take the trouble to come all the way round here to tell us! Sit down, Doctor, let me make you a cup of tea. Gary ain't in—he's got a temporary job on the docks—just sweepin' up at the moment. They said when he's proved he's reliable, he can have a job as security guard. Have to have some trainin' for that. But, thank heaven, the police have nothin' on him. He's in the clear now. Oh, that is so wonderful!'

Sasha went back to the hospital, feeling warm and glad that she had taken the trouble to go round. But when she walked into the common-room she realised she was a celebrity, as her colleagues shouted and clapped and called her 'Lady Doctor Heroine', as it was splashed on the front page of the *Liverpool Echo*. She was placed on a chair, and brought a cup of coffee and a ham roll, while they asked questions about what it was like to be attacked. She tried to answer. 'I was terrified at first. But then I remembered what I'd been taught in classes . . .' Her voice trailed off as she remembered Joe, burly and confident in his green track-suit, pretending to be a mugger and creeping up behind them, only to have them collapse on the coconut matting in giggles because he was pulling such funny faces to make himself menacing . . .

It was Pat Moore, Adam's registrar, who took her arm, gave her a paper handkerchief, and offered to take her back to her flat. 'No, thank you. I've got to go and see Joe.'

'Later. Get some rest.' And he was so kind and thoughtful that she forgave him for labelling her 'no fun' when Adam had first mentioned her. She went to bed and slept soundly all afternoon, the reaction from all the emotional upset finally catching up with her, so that it was getting dark when she woke.

'Adam! I said I'd see Adam at five!' She looked at her watch. It was only four. She tidied herself and composed her features before setting out across the shadowy car park—now safer for the arrest of the prowler. She presented herself at Sister's office. 'Mr Harrington not here?'

'No, Doctor—but Joe's awake, if you want a word.'

She pushed open the door. Joe was sitting up in bed, and he beamed when he saw her. 'Come in, love. I'm for the chop on Friday, Harrington says.'

She kissed his cheek. 'I'll be there, Joe. He said I could be there.'

Joe's eyes were grateful. 'That's nice of you, kid.'

'I'll be there when you wake, I promise.'

'Thanks. You don't know what that means.'

She looked into his troubled, blank eyes. 'Perhaps I do, Joe.'

'I'm not nervous. I just want it to be over.'

'You're never frightened of anything, Joe.'

'Well, I'll need some luck on Friday.' He leaned back, obviously weary. She knew the drug therapy would make him tired. She waited until he was asleep, holding his hand tightly until his breathing was regular and deep.

Adam was in his room. He smiled as she came in, but it was a distant, polite smile. '"Lady Doctor Heroine,"' he said. 'I'll say you were! How do you feel now? Pat said you were upset.' He was making an effort to be clinically aloof. She began to suspect the worst. At her look, he didn't prolong the chat, but put a film on the desk for her to see. 'I'm afraid there will be problems, Sasha. The size of the tumour isn't as important as the blood-vessels that feed it. I may have to tie off the cerebral artery. You know what it means?'

'Paralysis. Left-sided paraplegia. A wheelchair job.'

His voice had never been gentler. 'It's possible. But not inevitable.'

She was almost proud of her own composure, knowing what it could mean to both Joe and herself for the rest of their lives. 'But you will operate?'

'I have to. The tumour is taking too much space. I'll have to do it—hopefully remove it all, or if not, partially resect.'

'I know.'

He said, his voice still calm and eminently reasonable, giving her no opportunity to break down, 'You have time to come and watch?'

'Yes, I have. Thank you.'

There was a brief silence. She stood up to leave then, and Adam took a step towards her. 'I just wanted to say—that you may be making a big mistake, allowing yourself to be his prop, as it were.' He paused, but she said nothing. There was nothing to say. He went on, 'But I promise I'll say no more about it—it's none of my business. I—admire you very much, Sasha.'

'Don't. He wouldn't be in this mess if I'd been more sensible.'

He took an audible breath before saying, 'Shall we look on the bright side? I've done tumours as big as this before with no after-effects. Why not this time, too?'

She nodded and muttered, 'Please, Lord.' He turned away suddenly, and she looked up and met his gaze as he turned back. They both knew without words—and she just gave him a little nod of understanding before leaving the room and closing the door behind her. She stood for a moment, longing with all her heart to go back, where she knew he was waiting to soothe her, hold her . . . But only his skill could help her now. She had a mission, and there was nothing either of them could do that would alter that fact.

She was glad to go back to AED next day. Blessed work! She looked forward to the queue of irritable customers, with their trapped fingers and rusty nails in their feet. She dreaded more than anything having nothing to do with her hands, and so making time for thinking. But during a lull at lunchtime Sister Holloway said, 'You heard Dr Mortimer is getting himself engaged, Doctor?'

'Never!' Sasha managed a grin. 'You mean it?'

'Sure I do. They announced it at the Christmas party.'

Christmas . . . how far away, that white yacht and those emerald seas. Light years away in emotion and freedom and duty . . .

'Well, I'm delighted for him, and I hope they have a big wedding and invite us all.'

Sister said casually, 'I hear you spent the holiday with Mr Harrington.'

Sasha hooted with laughter. 'Just because someone borrows a man's villa doesn't mean they spent the holiday together, Sister! Gosh, how stories travel!'

'I guess they do, Doctor—I guess they do.'

She managed to sleep that night, though she woke several times with disturbed dreams, where both Joe and Adam figured as dark, unattainable figures on the far bank of a wild, rushing river. She had her bath, and ate a piece of orange for breakfast, her thoughts with Joe, who would have starved since midnight.

She went to see him before she changed into theatre greens. He lay on top of his bed, already gowned in white, drowsy from his premeds, his head encased in a white cap, although his hair was to be shaved as soon as he was on the table. She forced a smile and went forward to take his hand. 'I'm here, my lad, so see that you behave yourself!'

He opened his eyes and squeezed her hand. 'Thanks for coming, Sasha—it makes all the difference, having you here. Thanks. I love you.'

She tried to say the words, but they wouldn't come. Instead she lifted his hand to her lips and kissed it.

She heard Adam's voice in the corridor talking to Pat Moore, and she gripped Joe's hand even tighter. Adam was changed, though without cap and mask. He nodded to Sasha, saying heartily to Joe, 'Ready, old man? They are coming in a couple of minutes. Anything you'd like to say to me? Don't worry now—we'll do the very best we can.'

'I know that.'

Adam stood in the doorway, chatting to the registrar and the sister for a moment, while Joe still clung to Sasha's hand as they heard the clank of the trolley coming to take him along to theatre. There was a young nurse with the trolley, who was very sweet and gentle, saying in Joe's ear, 'Just think of it as a free haircut, my dear.'

And then he was on the table, anaesthetised, the tube in his lungs to breathe for him. Sasha gowned herself and crept in after him, looking down on the still form. Adam strode in, the one man who could help Joe. He turned to the anaesthetist. 'Everything OK your end, Harry?'

'Yes, over to you, Adam.'

'Then let's start. Would you pass the shaver, Sister? And the scalpel? Thank you.' And Sasha watched his hands, mesmerised.

CHAPTER EIGHT

IT WAS six hours later; Sasha's shoulders were aching and her eyes were sore after staring at all the delicate work Adam Harrington had carried out, with never a cross word or a slip of his talented fingers. But she still felt for Adam as he straightened his back and stretched out his arms as the registrar inserted the last stitch in the scalp wound, and arranged a drainage tube at the side of Joe's head. Adam moved back from the table and, as Sasha didn't move, he said gently, 'I've done what I can. There's no tumour left. I was as gentle as I could be with the surrounding structures—but you saw yourself how squashed the brain had been in the left frontal region.'

She stood up straight, moving her neck from side to side where it had stiffened. 'I know. I'm grateful.'

He said softly, 'I should get out of that gown if I were you, into something normal—he'll want to see something pretty when he opens his eyes.'

Pat Moore peeled off his gloves. 'I know I'd be pleased enough to see Dr Norton when I opened my eyes!'

Adam pulled down his mask, recognising the need to lighten the tension for all of them. 'Naturally enough.' The theatre sister supervised the porters as they pushed Joe's prostrate form along the corridor to Recovery. Pat left them. Sasha and Adam were alone in the empty theatre. He said, 'Aren't you going to change?'

'Yes. Of course.'

They were standing about a yard apart, neither of them moving. It was quiet in the corridor outside the theatre. She saw something like pity in Adam's eyes, and he said, 'It's all right. I'm not going to tell you anything. It's your life, Sasha. I think sometimes doctors think they can direct others' lives, just because we have the ability to

119

save a few. I won't try it with you, my dear.' He
smoothed his fingers through his hair, and pulled off his
cap. 'Go to Joe. He'll be looking for you.'

'Shouldn't you ask me if I want to talk to you? You do
that with all the other relatives.'

'You're not a relative.' Adam's answer was curt. He
turned away, but looked back at her before he left the
theatre. Sasha watched the swinging door, and felt
nothing but gratitude and affection for Adam. He had
undoubtedly saved Joe's life. And she knew he would be
there if she needed anyone to talk to. She lowered her
head as she walked to the changing-room. One day, if she
passed her exams, she would be in such a position—
where other people hung on your every word. She pulled
on her skirt and jumper. If she ever made it to consultant
surgeon, there was only one model she would have
followed. And even as she walked along to Recovery she
knew she could never admire any man as much as she
admired Adam Harrington.

She paused at the entrance to Recovery. There was a
figure already by Joe's bed, and she paused before she
recognised the white-coated shape of Barbie Green, who
was standing back to allow the sister to take his blood
pressure and adjust his oxygen mask. As the sister moved
away Barbie went back to Joe's bandaged head. She
looked up as Sasha came in, and her smile was broad.
'He's OK. No paralysis. Just watch his fingers and toes!'
And she leaned over Joe, whispering to him to show
Sasha. She lifted the blanket, and Joe slowly bent his toes
downwards and back. 'Isn't it wonderful? He's made it!
How lucky can anyone get? Well done, Joe!'

Sasha leaned forward to speak to him as his eyelids
flickered and opened to recognise her. 'Well done, Joe.'
She whispered Joe's name, but she thought of Adam's
morning of toil to produce this miracle. She had
watched every move Adam had made inside Joe's head.
And, although she told Joe he had done well, it was
Adam she was praising. How he had managed to
remove a tumour that size without harming any blood-

vessels or nerves was still amazing her. She rejoiced for Joe—but she venerated Adam. Yet as she stood close to the helpless form, surrounded by tubes and drips, she felt a great sense of responsibility. Joe had suffered greatly—and, if she had been the doctor she thought she was, she would have recognised that he needed help—and made sure he got it. It was just an enormous stroke of luck—and Adam's enormous skill—that had saved Joe to live a normal life. Sasha had nothing to be proud of. She had allowed his condition to worsen without seeking help. She sank slowly on the seat beside her long-time friend. 'Joe?'

He looked at her, and smiled under the oxygen mask. 'Sasha, love? I feel as though I've been lost in a wad of cotton wool, and I've just come out. Already I feel my mind clearing. It's a miracle, Sasha.'

'I know.' She reached for his hand under the blankets, and squeezed it. Barbie stood at the foot of the bed, her face a picture of joy. Just then the doors swung open, and Adam and Pat Moore came in, followed by a retinue of distinguished visitors. Adam hardly spoke to the girls as he continued explaining to his guests what procedures he had followed in Joe's operation. There was a chorus of congratulation as Adam demonstrated movement in Joe's four limbs.

Adam held up his hand to stem the congratulations. He beckoned Sasha to join them as he said, 'The next twenty-four hours are crucial. This is where the nurses are just as important as the surgeon. Any sign of a seizure, and I must be informed at once.' His eyes met Sasha's, implying that he knew she would be at Joe's side. 'At once, please. And Doctor, if you would keep an eye on the drainage tube?''

'I will. Thank you, sir.' Their eyes met again for a single second before Adam turned away to show his guests another patient. Sasha didn't look after him. Instead she looked down at Joe. This was where her future lay. Thank heaven, he would be able to go back to work and again become the happy-go-lucky physio who was so popular with everyone. She would always be at his side—because that was where she should have been when he had become so sick.

Joe shivered suddenly—and didn't seem able to stop. She called Sister. 'Can we wrap him in foil? His temperature is low.'

The nurses brought the silver sheet that helped to prevent a body cooling down. Sasha helped tuck it in, meanwhile keeping an eye on the blood-stained fluid draining from his head, and the oxygen mask rising and falling with comforting regularity. She put Joe's hand under the blankets, and leaned her head on her arms on the bed.

She was wakened by Barbie shaking her. 'Wake up, Sasha. Time you went and got yourself something to eat. I bet you had no lunch.'

'What time is it? Sasha shook her head and looked down at Joe's sleeping form. She looked across at the nurse. 'Everything in order?' The nurse nodded and smiled. 'Why didn't you wake me?'

She said, 'Mr Harrington told me to let you sleep.'

Barbie patted her shoulder. 'Come on, Sasha. You can't go on duty like that. Go and eat something hot. I'm finished for the day. I'll sit with him until seven or eight.'

'But'—I ought to be here.' Sasha stood up, stiff and sleepy, and looked lovingly at Joe.

Barbie said softly, 'He's my friend too, Sasha. And I'm not dropping on my feet!'

Sasha said, 'My, what a change in you, Barbie! So efficient and full of energy. That holiday has done you good.'

Barbie nodded. 'And I've eaten. Now, be sensible. You're on night duty, and you can't sit here and do it.' And as Sasha acknowledged this, Barbie said, 'And don't come back tonight. Adam popped in and said Joe needed to sleep. Too many people from his department wanted to come, and he isn't allowing any visitors until tomorrow. And he said ring before you come.'

'I understand.' Sasha walked downstairs deep in thought. She knew that Joe needed to rest—but why ban her from visiting? He had said he wouldn't interfere—yet surely just sitting by the bed wouldn't harm Joe? She turned into the mess. In spite of missing lunch, she didn't feel like eating, but knew it would be silly not to. She ordered a plate of asparagus soup, and sipped it slowly, until the final mouthful was almost cold. Life was strange. In the space of one day Joe Acourt had been brought back from almost certain death by the skill of Adam Harrington. Adam was the one who had recognised Joe's symptoms, and persuaded him to come in for examination. Joe—and therefore Sasha—would be indebted to Adam for as long as they lived.

She walked into Casualty, to be greeted by Sister Holloway and the three nurses all asking about Joe, and she was so relieved to be able to give them good news. 'No paralysis. Should make a complete recovery.'

Sister said, 'He's a good fellow.'

'Joe or Adam?'

Sister smiled at her, her white teeth making a clean split in the sweet dark face. 'I meant Joe, my dear—but I can't deny it goes for Mr Harrington too. And I think I see where your thoughts are just now. You are thinking what a great thing it is to be a surgeon, eh? Or are you just thinking what a handsome face your surgeon has?'

Sasha turned away. 'Now, Sister, I don't want us to fall out, so don't ever say things like that again.' She took a deep breath at the hurt look on Sister's face, and apologised at once. 'I'm not myself just now.'

'I know that. Think nothing of it.' And at that moment there was a jumble of voices at the door, and an ambulanceman called, 'Is the doctor there? There's a child here swallowed a plum-stone.'

Sasha sprang into action, and got the frightened mother to carry the girl on to a bed. 'Did she choke?'

'Yes, Doctor—she was turning blue, but she's quiet

now. It must have just gone down.'

Sasha spoke soothingly. 'If it's in the stomach, then she won't come to any harm just now. Let's listen to her chest.' There was no abnormality. Sasha got the child to drink some water, which she did with no difficulty. Sasha signed an X-ray form. 'Let's take a photo of that stone.' She smiled at the girl. 'Chest and abdomen, Sister.' And as the patient was taken away, she said to the nurse, 'She may have lacerated the oesophagus—but it can't be too bad or she'd have cried when she took the drink.'

More patients presented themselves, and Sasha was kept busy until about eleven. Then a familiar figure came in. 'Any coffee going?'

'Barbie! What are you doing here?'

'Going home, actually. I've been sitting with Joe.'

'But—Adam said no one——'

Barbie said firmly, 'I knew you'd feel better if someone stayed. He didn't wake, except just to take his anticonvulsants and his steroids.'

Sasha looked at Barbara curiously. Why had she stayed so long? 'It's very nice of you . . .'

Barbie grinned. 'And why not? He's my friend too, you know.'

'Yes—of course he is.'

Just then the night porter came into the office, tapping on the door first, and saying, 'Present for you, Doc—it's not tickin'—I checked.' He handed Sasha a square package. 'Sent by messenger from the Atlantic Tower Hotel.' He winked. 'I'd change places with him any time!' He grinned and saluted, and took his Liverpool humour back to the lodge.

Sasha pulled off the plain gold wrapper, Barbara watching curiously. 'I don't know anyone staying at the Atlantic Tower.' She uncovered a box lined with tissue strands, and drew out a tin of caviare, a tin of Greek sardines, the big luscious kind, and two small bottles, one containing ouzo and the other eoliki, the almond liqueur. The girls looked at each other. They had

sampled all these goodies on board the *Dolphin* at
Christmas—but had hardly expected to find any here.
'The Atlantic Tower?' repeated Sasha, and searched for
some clue as to the sender. At the bottom of the box was
a small card edged with gold. It read 'To help you pass a
couple of long, lonely nights. Will be in touch soon.
Yours, JS.'

Barbie said, 'John Steadman? In Liverpool? But
why?'

'I can't think. Unless—oh, Barbie, I heard Adam
recommend one of his patients to Alex to do the interior
design of his new holiday complex. Cheaper than
London prices, he said. I bet he sent John to
investigate!'

Barbara said, 'I do hope I'm invited to stay and help
you eat it.'

'Sure. Nip to the mess and pinch some crackers.
Good old John.'

Barbara was soon back with a tin-opener and a packet
of crackers. 'I wonder if John volunteered to come.
Remember what Andreas said about him not wanting to
be beaten? Wouldn't it be exciting if he's pursuing you,
Sasha?' She levered the top from the caviare tin. 'Do
you think Sister would like some? There's plenty.'

Sasha was staring into space suddenly. 'I hope John
hasn't come for that reason. There's only Joe in my life
now, and I want that made very clear.'

Barbie paused in the act of opening the biscuits. 'Who
are you kidding?' she said quietly. 'You're crazy about
that guy.' There was no need to name him. They both
knew who she was talking about.

Sasha said thoughtfully, 'I'm sure there are lots of
women who are attracted to men without expecting
anything to come of the feeling. That's how it is with me
and Adam. It will pass off eventually.'

Barbara looked at her, her blue eyes wide and serious.
Then she decided that no good would be served by
continuing with the subject. 'Well—do I get any of your
caviare or not?'

'Sorry, Barbie—help yourself. Pass that tumbler and I'll give you some eoliki.'

'None for you?'

'I'm on duty. Anyway . . . I can't give myself a midnight feast when poor Joe is lying up there . . .' Even though he was making excellent progress, her conscience was troubling her—that all Joe's problems were her fault, and that it had taken Adam Harrington not only to spot the illness, but also to cure it.

Sister tapped on the door. 'Dr Norton, a query appendix case from a 999 call.'

Barbie stood up and drained her glass. 'I'll be off and leave you to it. See you.' She left on light feet, with a cheery wave, and Sasha watched her for a moment, delighted at the change in her, at the disappearance of her depression. Then Sasha went to see to the patient, a young girl of fourteen with typical symptoms of appendicitis. She called the surgical registrar with an apology for the lateness of the hour.

'What will you give me if I come and see her?' he joked.

'How does caviare grab you?'

'Honest? I'm on my way.' And the young surgeon helped himself to a mouthful before going in to admit his patient.

It had been a long day. Sasha got to bed at four, slept solidly until midday, and woke with her anxiety over Joe still strong in her mind. She cooked herself scrambled eggs, having eaten little the previous day. By that time she began to feel more confident that Joe would be feeling better, and she wrapped herself up and walked across the frosty car park and took the lift to Nelson Ward. Sister was in her office, and Sasha knocked politely. 'Afternoon, Sister. May I see Mr Acourt?'

Sister hesitated. Sasha saw her look up, and as she stuck her head further into the office she realised that Adam was there, going through some X-rays. 'I say, I'm sorry. I'll wait outside.'

'Come in, Dr Norton.' Adam's voice was cool, detached. Sister stood up, sensing a private discussion, and excused herself. Adam said, 'I'm told John Steadman is in town.'

'So I believe.'

'Why?'

She looked up into the grey eyes under the dark eyebrows. 'Does it matter? It's nothing to do with me.' Then she realised he thought it was. 'Adam, you don't think—surely not—that I'm encouraging him? How could you, when you know I'm worried sick over Joe?'

He turned away suddenly and looked down at his X-rays without seeing them. 'I'm sorry. That man has a strange effect on me.'

'I remember.' The sight of John spreadeagled on the deck, and Adam gently massaging his knuckles, was vivid in her mind.

Adam allowed himself a slight smile. 'Joe's doing well.'

'Thank goodness.'

'I'll come along with you.' He replaced the films in their envelope and placed the envelope on Sister's desk with his customary precision. He said casually, 'So you have no plans to see John?'

'None whatsoever.'

He led the way along the corridor, then waited for her to draw level, but they didn't speak, and she sensed his relief. She longed to touch his arm, to be in contact with him physically, as though she drew strength from him like electricity, from this gentle, all-powerful person who had so bewitched her senses . . .

Joe was sitting up and the bandages had been removed from his head, so that the long row of stitches across his naked scalp showed up vividly with the yellow of the iodine. His grin was broad, however, and he sat erect, all drainage tubes gone and no sign of drips or oxygen. 'Hello, Sasha, love. How do I look? Last of the Mohicans, eh?' And he held out his arms. She went to him wordlessly and Adam turned away, leaving them together. Joe held her for a long time, until he said into her hair, 'I bet you thought I'd gone forever. That's what it feels like, Sasha—that I've been away from you. A long way away.'

She drew back to look into his face. 'Yes, Joe—even without your hair, it's the old Joe I can see in your eyes, not that stranger we all grew to fear.'

'I know I hit you,' he said quietly. 'I've been odd—and I've been cruel.' He reached for her hand. 'I've always despised blokes who hit women.'

'That's forgotten.'

'Not yet. You were trying to help me too—I see that now.'

Sasha squeezed his hand. 'Forget it. I have.' To change the subject she said, 'You heard about the way I dealt with that prowler, did you?'

He pretended to be annoyed. 'How on earth did a pupil of mine allow a puny attacker to get so near? That's what I want to know!'

'It won't happen again, sir,' she smiled.

'I know it won't, love, because from now on I'll be around to look after you. I'll make sure of that.' He took her hand in both of his and said, 'You mean the world to me, you know that, don't you?'

'I won't let you down, Joe. I promise.'

'You mean that, sweetheart?'

She looked into his eyes. 'I mean it.'

'I love you, you know.' And Sasha hated herself for not being able to say it back to him, as she laid her cheek on his bare chest and prayed she would be forgiven for living a lie. Time would change that. She could grow to love him in time. After a while, she said, 'Now that you are all right, I can get back to my studies. I couldn't concentrate before.'

She was right. The moving experience of watching Adam's healing hands bringing Joe back from certain death had inspired her ambition as well as her love, and she knew with all her heart that she wanted to do that, to be a surgeon with that kind of power and skill. So she went back to her work with renewed vigour, visiting Joe once a day, but allowing nothing to interfere with her evenings. She would spread her histology plates all over the floor, sit on the sofa with her notes, and memorise each question she thought she might be asked. If she met Adam in the ward she was polite, but made sure she avoided any tête-à-tête with him, knowing it would unsettle her resolve too much.

One night there was a knock at the door. Thinking it might be Barbie, she picked her way through her strewn papers, not bothering to tidy her hair or smooth her rumpled jeans and sweater. She opened the door—and her eyes widened in amazement and apprehension. 'Adam!' And then she said, 'Joe's all right, isn't he?'

'He's fine.' Adam was wearing casual trousers, and a pullover over an open-necked shirt, and his eyes looked at her closely with that look which always made her heart leap. 'It's you I'm worried about.'

'There's—no need.'

'You've lost weight.' He paused. 'May I come in?'

'Yes—of course. But my Primary is in a couple of weeks . . .' She led the way in. 'I'm afraid I'm frantically untidy.' She found her breath coming in short bursts, and tried to control her sudden panic. Why should Adam come here now? 'I—thought you had visitors.'

Adam sat down on one of the armchairs. 'Too much reading isn't good for you. You get stale, and you don't absorb what you are reading.'

Sasha looked down ruefully at the floor and nodded. 'You're right, of course.'

'Have you eaten?'

'I was just going to heat some soup.'

'I see.' And as he said no more, but waited for her to look up at him, she faced him and reddened at her lie. He said gently, 'I thought we could have dinner. It would do you good—and it would make me very happy.'

He seemed to be sincere. But then, Adam was always sincere. And as he caught her look and held it she found herself thinking how differently they felt about each other now—no longer consultant and house officer, but close—as friends who understood one another and had a link of honesty and intimacy. It had started in the Greek villa on Christmas night. Whatever happened in her life, that night would perhaps always be the one she remembered most, treasured most.

He said, 'You're very quiet.'

'I was just remembering Zaramos.'

'So was I.' And he rose suddenly and crossed the small, untidy rug to sit beside her on the sofa, one hand resting round her shoulders. 'It was like this.' And he drew her close so that his head was touching her hair.

She felt a frisson of excitement, but she said, trying to keep her voice firm, 'But things are different now for us.'

'Who is making them different?'

She looked down, but couldn't say Joe's name, as Adam moved his thigh closer to hers and smoothed back her hair from her forehead, so that he could kiss her very gently. 'Don't tie yourself down. You're too young, and you know it, don't you, Sasha?'

She didn't answer. His lips moved from her forehead to her cheek, and then found her mouth, waiting and hungry for him. She didn't know how it happened, only that she was deeply unhappy, and that being with Adam Harrington was the only thing that could take away the pain. In spite of Joe, in spite of Adam's reputation, she found herself putting her arms round his hard body and allowing herself to be embraced and held like something precious and loved. As he murmured her name she clung to him, wanting the moment to go on forever.

'Is this why you really came?' she asked breathlessly, resting her cheek against his chest.

'I came to make sure you are a woman, and not a Girl Guide.' He found her lips again, and their kiss was long and deep and thrilling. After a long time he whispered, 'Have I convinced you? Just because you are a damn good doctor and have an exam to pass, it doesn't mean you are a robot, you know.'

'I think I know that now.' Alarm bells in her mind were trying to tell her that Adam Harrington was a loner who broke women's hearts. But her body was ignoring them, very conscious now of his male hardness pressing into her stomach as they lay on the sofa, limbs entwined, caring nothing for the rumpled medical notes around them, nor for the fact that no more had been said about going out for dinner. She said quietly, 'I've never—you know . . .'

Adam's voice was very tender. 'I do know. I'm not a brute, you know. You can send me away now, if you want to. But ever since Christmas, I've wanted to show you who you are, Sasha—I didn't want you to learn from just anyone.'

She reached for his lips then, wanting more. And as he bent and satisfied her she held him close, and knew that never in her life had Joe meant so much as this man who now possessed her body and her spirit. He was right. That Christmas night they had shared their minds and memories with one another. Tonight they shared more. It seemed right and good, and too powerful to deny.

It was very late when Adam said, 'My dear, I'm going to insist that I cook you a meal. Show me your fridge.'

Lying on her back, her hair over her eyes, Sasha murmured, 'It's far too late—see—it's past midnight! And I'm not hungry at all.'

He smiled and kissed her again, before scrambling up and going to the kitchen. She heard him opening cupboards, then she heard the mixer. She couldn't let him cook for her! She rubbed her eyes, straightened her clothes, and followed him to the stove, where he was just pouring beaten eggs into a pan. 'Scrambled eggs and bacon. Any tinned mushrooms?'

Sasha put her arms around him from behind and leaned her cheek against his muscular back, smelling the warmth of his body in the cashmere sweater. 'There might be. Does it matter?' And he turned round, embraced her and ruffled her hair, before kissing it and pulling her head back for a kiss on her ready mouth.

'You are so lovely,' he whispered. But a hiss from the pan made him turn round just in time to stop the bacon burning. 'You're to eat up all this, you know.'

Sasha smiled. 'Then you must stay and make sure I do.'

'I intend to.' His voice was deep and gentle, and his smile made her heart sing.

Sasha didn't know when Adam left her flat. But when she woke in the morning the sky was cold and grey, and she knew that reality had come back. She couldn't regret what had happened. She felt alive and warm and somehow very wise. Yet as she picked up her papers and notes and arranged them neatly, and then found a clean white coat, ready for work, she steeled herself for what she knew she must do—stick with Joe Acourt, and treat Adam Harrington as a friend. He was kind, sincere, handsome—everything a man should be. But he never stayed with any woman. And Sasha must never let herself forget it. Lifting her chin, she locked the flat door behind her, and walked purposefully across towards Casualty.

CHAPTER NINE

JOE was better, much better, and a great favourite with his nurses. Sasha saw him every day, but he was constantly inundated with friends and colleagues from his own department, as well as Barbie Green, so she was able to get down to her studies with greater concentration. Sasha had not seen Adam to speak to since that night they had shared, which was helpful for her peace of mind. However, she had to go to the personnel office for a form to regain her Primary expenses one morning, and found herself bumping into him—literally—in the doorway.

She murmured a greeting, and was about to continue on her way when he said, 'Has Joe any relatives, Sasha?'

She paused, surprised. 'Not in Liverpool. Why didn't you ask him?' Then she felt afraid. 'There's no problem, is there? He is getting on all right?' She was grateful to him for showing no flicker of emotion.

'Yes, quite well. Only there's always the possibility of convulsions, as well as headaches. And, of course, he won't be allowed to drive for twelve months. I can leave it to you, can I, to see to returning his licence? He'll have to have a regular yearly review.'

He was treating her like a relative, making sure she knew all about Joe's future. She accepted it quietly, though she felt Adam was rubbing it in a bit. 'The driving isn't a problem while he's working here. When he wants to start his own business, he should be better.'

'I see. He's going private. Well, good luck.' From Adam's detachment, she could have been just any casual patient's relative.

'Thank you. And thank you for all you've done for

him.'

He put his hand on her arm in a friendly but distant way. 'All in a day's work, my dear.' And he turned away to speak to one of his colleagues without even saying goodbye.

She stood for a moment, watching him disappear into the operating suite. He couldn't be jealous of Joe, surely? He was just making sure he didn't hurt her—like the kind person he was. Adam Harrington was jealous of no one. He was a loner who had got used to his loneliness. She sighed deeply. If only she didn't dream about him sometimes, wake up holding her own arms and know he was only a dream lover, and that reality lay with a totally different man.

Her studies were almost at an end. Her train ticket to Edinburgh was booked, and she felt herself ready to face the Royal College of Surgeons. The night before she left she paid her customary visit to Joe. But she felt apprehensive when she reached his room and found it occupied by Adam and Pat Moore, as well as the sister and another nurse. It was the nurse who went to her outside the door. 'He's just had a small fit. Nothing serious, just a momentary loss of concentration.'

'Will I be allowed in?' Sasha's heart contracted.

'Oh, yes. I'll ask Mr Harrington, shall I?' She went back inside the room. No one came out for a while, and Sasha stood clasping and unclasping her hands. Finally the entourage trooped out. Adam stopped to speak to her. 'Better let him sleep. Just stay five minutes.' He searched her face, and seemed unable to stop himself offering comfort. 'I've changed his drug therapy. I doubt if it will happen again.'

'Yes.' Her voice was small.

He said, 'See me before you leave.'

Joe was chirpy. 'It was only a little one,' he said with a grin. 'So you're off to Edinburgh tomorrow?'

'I'd rather stay with you.'

'No need, love. They treat me like a sultan in here.' He reached for her hand. 'You're too good to me, lass.'

She said fervently, 'Not good enough, Joe. It'll never be good enough.'

'Hey, don't say that. Now, you go and get a good night's sleep, and come and see me when you get back. All the luck in the world, my love.'

She left him to sleep, and walked slowly along the corridor towards Adam's room. She tapped gently on the door and went in. He was alone. 'I know I promised to say nothing, but I feel I have to have a talk with you. You're going to Edinburgh tomorrow?'

'Yes. Multiple choice on Monday morning.'

'I know you ought to pass—but this sort of distraction won't have helped.' He stood up and came round the desk towards her and her heart contracted. 'Devoting yourself to Joe won't help either. It won't help him, Sasha—he's got to be independent.'

'Not right away. He needs me just now.' Her eyes pleaded with him to understand.

'Sasha—be sensible. Do you want a strong, proud man leaning on you? I'm advising you from my own experience. Do you understand, Sasha?'

'Your experience?' she echoed. 'You mean— your—wife?'

'Yes.' He went over and closed the door. 'I've never talked of it to anyone before.' He sat on the corner of the desk and gestured her to sit down on the chair near him—so near she could smell the fresh cotton of his shirt, the tweed of his jacket. 'When Deborah was ill I—more or less gave up all my activities and friends to stay with her. It was only when she was dying that she told me it had made her feel more guilty and upset because she knew I had no one to turn to. She had wanted me to carry on my normal life, so that she knew I could carry on afterwards. As it was——' he faced her for the first time—'I had to take six months off before I could face a normal life again.'

There was a silence. Sasha looked up into that well-known, well-loved face, the eyebrows drawn straight across hooded eyes as he relived the strain of that time, felt again the sadness. Suddenly she put out a hand and touched him, unable to prevent herself. He caught hers in both of his and held it, struggling with emotion. After a while she said, 'I can't just stop visiting him.'

'You can stop babying him.'

'I'll try.'

'Keep it light. Don't treat him all the time as though you were his mother——'

'Or his wife?'

Adam let her hand drop and turned back to his desk. 'I've told you before, such a move would be—utter cruelty—not only to him, but to you. It would be a wicked act.'

She could almost touch the tension in the room. To ease it, she said quickly, 'Well, as long as he's all right, then there's nothing else on my mind except that exam.'

He faced her, went to her, and they shook hands. 'Good luck, Sasha. Don't forget—you've got a friend here—someone to talk to if you need to.'

She nodded. She felt his breath on her cheek, and longed to move closer, to feel the comfort of his arms about her . . . 'I'll try and come back with good news.' She fumbled with the door-handle, wanting to get away before he saw her eyes filling.

She tidied her books and put away her slides, but her thoughts were not about work, but about Adam and his wife Deborah. It must have been a terrible ordeal for him to live through. It had been Andreas who had been with him through that time. Andreas and Artemis . . .

Barbie came down to wish her luck. She carried paper bags full of fruit and chocolates. 'Just taking these to Joe. Don't worry about him. I'll make sure he doesn't feel neglected.'

On the train it was the same—she wanted to study, but her mind dwelt only on the two men she had left behind. Little things, like that little red spot on Joe's bare chest, that she had meant to mention to the houseman. She began to think of the differential diagnosis of little red spots, and started to get worried because she was stuck on a train with no access to a telephone, and Joe might need more treatment . . . So worked up did she get that by the time she reached Edinburgh she had forgotten all exam nerves, and only thought of finding an unoccupied phone on the draughty cold station. She waited, tapping her feet to keep them warm while the switchboard bleeped Nelson Ward. The houseman finally answered. 'Spot? Yes, there are more. We noticed them this morning. We're waiting for Mr Harrington.'

'Don't give him any more anticonvulsants. I think he's allergic to the new drugs—you'll have to find an alternative——'

'Housemen don't tell men like Harrington what to do, Sasha.'

'Think of some polite way to suggest it, then. For goodness——' But her money had run out, and she had no more change.

A strange bedroom, a cold environment, worry about Joe—it was little surprise that she couldn't study that night, and slept badly when she went to bed. All the same, as she walked into the sombre examination hall she felt justified in believing she knew a fair amount of the subjects she had been studying. After the exam, the young doctors got together in a bar in Princes Street and swapped ideas and hints on what might come up in the next papers.

The next day there were slides to identify, and more cases to describe. Sasha worked steadily, refusing to allow herself to be ruffled when a couple of slides mystified her. Afterwards, she didn't stay for the post-mortem, but hurried along Princes Street, hoping to catch an earlier train. She was just in time, and leaned back breathlessly in her seat, drained of all thought and all emotion. How could she fail, when she knew her stuff? All she needed to do now was to get to Liverpool and watch the post for the summons to the viva voce exams, which would be sent to all those who had reached a decent standard in their written work.

When they reached Preston, she missed the connection to Liverpool. She sat in a draughty waiting-room, sipping bitter coffee, and wondering just how much she wanted to be a surgeon. It appeared to be an obstacle course even to take the exams. By the time she reached the Western, she was freezing and exhausted and it was after midnight.

There was no letter from Edinburgh next morning. Or the morning after. Sasha had hoped that she had passed, in spite of the mistakes she had made with the slides. But on the third day she had to admit that she had failed her first attempt at the Primary Fellowship. That morning, as she saw the postman ride away without leaving her the notice she was looking for—the summons to return to Edinburgh to take the vivas—she knew this was going to be the hardest day of her life, as she met her friends and colleagues in turn, and admitted that she had failed. It was the first exam she had failed in her whole life.

They were all kind, encouraging, sure she would pass the next time. She dreaded most of all meeting Adam—but the day was fortunate in that she never saw him, not even when she went up to tell Joe. Joe was unconcerned. 'My fault, love—you were preoccupied with my problem. You'll easily get it next time. Apply now—apply to the Glasgow one—that's next month, isn't it?'

'Never mind me—How are you, dear?'

Joe opened his pyjama jacket to reveal the last of the rash that had so bothered her while she was away. 'The houseman was great—told Harrington he understood that some drugs can cause this reaction. Harrington changed the anticonvulsants right away.' He buttoned it up. 'I must say, I felt a bit of a mess—had a temperature, too.'

Sasha was just about to sympathise when she remembered what Adam had warned, and instead she said, 'Just be glad you're getting another few days in bed. In this weather, we all envy you!'

'I've no choice.'

She went away sadly. She had wanted to mother him, to make him feel that she cared, yet so deeply had Adam's warning sunk in that she dared not. She went back to her flat, and curled up with a romance while great storm clouds built up outside, and rain came down from them. The phone rang during a loud gust of wind, and she had to wait to make sure she had heard it. 'Hello?'

'Adam here. Want to talk?'

Her heart sank. 'I failed. What else is there to say?' He didn't answer, so she added, 'But it's nice of you to ring.'

He said shortly, 'I rang Phillips.'

'The Prof in Edinburgh? Why?'

'I didn't believe you could fail. So I asked him.'

'You didn't!'

'I had to know, Sasha.' She felt warm and grateful for that. Adam went on, 'He said you passed everything, and were only slightly shaky on the slides—borderline, in fact, but there were just so many borderlines they could take—so you only missed by a whisker.'

'Oh, Adam. You're so kind.'

'Well, I thought you'd like to know. Makes it easier to apply to Glasgow, doesn't it?'

'I will, of course. I'll ring first thing for a form.'

'OK. And see me in four years about that job!'

She smiled herself. 'I won't hold you to that, Adam.' She rang off, feeling ten feet tall. And if Adam Harrington had been there he would almost have been hugged, so glad was she to hear his news. She suddenly ran downstairs to Barbie's flat. 'Come on—let's go to town! I feel like lunch out.'

On the way in, Barbie said, 'I'm very fond of Joe, you know.'

'Everyone is.'

'I wanted you to know—I might go into business with him. We've been talking it over. He needs a driver—and

I need a nine-to-five job. I could do a year's osteopathy. I've checked.'

Sasha said, 'So you've passed the planning stage, then? That was quick.' And she wondered why Joe hadn't mentioned anything to her.

'Do you mind? If I work with Joe, I mean?' Barbie sounded hesitant.

Sasha pulled herself together. 'Mind? It would be great to have both my best friends working together.' And as they went into a café and ordered espressos—'in memory of Zaramos'—she raised her cup to Barbie and said, 'Here's to dreams coming true!'

'And yours, Sasha.' But Sasha was thinking about her dream lover then, not her ambition to be a surgeon, and she blushed and changed the subject. 'We'll be able to take him home the day after tomorrow,' added Barbie. 'I thought of doing some shopping for him as a coming home present.'

Sasha smiled. 'Then I'll cook the meal. What do you think he'd like?'

'Steak pie and Brussels sprouts. He said hospital food has made him yearn for steak pie from Satter-thwaites.'

'Then steak pie he shall have.' It was nice to have something happy to do, and the girls tidied Joe's large Victorian flat and filled the vases with spring flowers in time for the triumphal return.

It was a splendid meal, with Joe in great spirits, joking and laughing, as well as appreciating all they had done for him. 'I'll be on sick pay for a while. I thought maybe I'll decorate the upper floor and let it out for a bit of extra cash.'

'Good idea. Occupational therapy as well.'

'I'm no weakling, Sasha. I'm back to my training, you know. Just not allowed to do press-ups in case I get headaches!'

As the girls left, he called after them down the overgrown little path, 'I'll take you both out next Saturday.'

'It's a deal!' But as they walked back to the hospital, Barbie said, 'He's all alone now. Things are going to be different for him. No regular meals, people popping in, someone to remind him to take his tablets . . .'

'I'll visit every day. It's only ten minutes' walk.'

'Sasha, you've an exam to pass. Leave the visiting to me until after Glasgow.' And Sasha felt guilty because she felt so relieved not to have to see Joe so often. Poor Joe, who had been through so much. She had almost forgotten how much she had gone through before the operation, how much mental torment she had endured, rather than ditch him for good. She went back to her books and her slides, making sure that she could identify every histology picture in the book. She had no weak points now. She had mastered her work. If she were borderline before—then now there was no way she could be failed.

It was the weekend before she went to Glasgow when Philip Mortimer stopped her just as she was leaving Casualty. 'Sasha, love, I want you to meet my fiancée, Rachel. Can you come to a concert with us? Only she's a music teacher, and I need some moral support.'

'Why me?'

'You played the violin at school.' Philip looked almost sheepish—something unfamiliar to Sasha, so she paid attention. He admitted, 'And Rachel has been told I work with the most eligible bachelor-girl in the hospital, so I was hoping I could persuade you to come along in very plain clothes, no make-up and, if you could possibly manage it, glasses.'

Sasha hooted with laughter. 'I'll come, Philip. I do love music—and I'd adore to disguise myself just to prove to your beloved that there's no hanky-panky between us!'

'You don't know how grateful I am. It isn't that Rachel doesn't trust me. Only we got engaged without knowing much about each other—and I think she's getting hints of my—earlier reputation!'

'Your worries are over, friend. Not only will I turn

up, but I'll wear the glasses I was prescribed when I got headaches during A-levels. They're absolutely horrific!'

'You're sure you can spare the time?'

'Very sure. My revision is complete. I think an evening at the Philharmonic will do me good.'

'We're meeting at the pub opposite.'

'I'll be there—complete with Dame Edna glasses!'

Philip looked dubious. 'You don't have to overdo it,' he retorted with a worried frown.

She took the bus to the Philharmonic pub. It was crowded inside, but she had been there so often as a student that she knew which nook would be vacant. She was wearing absolutely no make-up, and her plainest black coat over her plainest old-fashioned skirt. She carried the magnifying glasses in her pocket—only prescribed because she had been working too hard during her A-levels. The frames curved upwards in a most unattractive way, and even for Philip Mortimer's peace of mind she couldn't bear to wear them until absolutely necessary.

'Hello, Sasha.' She swung round sharply, hating the idea of meeting anyone she knew in such an unattractive outfit. Then she gasped to see Adam, seated at a small table, with two halves of lager in front of him. 'I'm glad you're here first. I was hoping you would be.'

She went up to him, feeling ridiculous. 'I— I . . .'

'You're sweet. You're helping Philip impress Rachel. That's why I'm here, too.'

She saw the funny side, and started to giggle. 'I must look so stupid.'

'No. You look like a very earnest student, Sasha. But with your face, you couldn't look stupid if you tried.' Adam himself was wearing a dark suit and no tie, and he looked years younger than she knew he must be. 'It's my box we're using tonight. So, you see, you aren't the only one roped in to back up our friend Philip's proposal.'

She sat at the table, laughing with relief. 'I do hope they make the engagement official soon. This could become a strain!' She sipped the drink gratefully. When she put it down, she said, 'I haven't thanked you yet for your phone call after I failed my exam. Who told you I'd failed?'

'You did.'

'I didn't. I told no one until they asked.'

Adam smiled. 'I was looking out for you. I waited in the department, where I have a view of the residences. I knew from the way you walked, Sasha—dragging your bag. I didn't ring then, but, my dear, I do know what it feels like.'

She faced him, feeling a great love for the man who had stayed in his room for a sight of a bedraggled female coming back at the dead of night. She said stoutly, 'You won't see such a sight next time.'

He grinned. 'I hope not.' And Sasha looked away, overwhelmed by his caring, by his sensitivity, not ringing when he'd understood she wouldn't want to talk . . . There could never be another Adam.

The happy couple arrived, breathless and pink-faced. 'No parking spaces,' puffed Philip, who was not looking forward to an evening of Rossini, Beethoven and Britten. Sasha took out her glasses, with a sidelong look at Adam, who behaved perfectly. But while the other two were deciding what to have to drink he gave her a very big wink. She responded with a smile. This was a new situation to be in with someone she adored. And, from the outset, it promised to be a lot of fun. She had encountered the caring side of Adam. And in Zaramos, the romantic side—and she knew the passionate side, too . . . But now it appeared that, when necessary, the great surgeon possessed a puckish and delightful sense of humour, and she felt excited at the thought of testing it out.

Rachel de Caux Routledge appeared irritated with Philip's suggestion as to what they should drink. Sasha beckoned them over. 'We're having Rossini first—I always find Chablis just right before Rossini.'

She had given Adam a look before she spoke. She was thrilled by his perfect response—as though they had rehearsed their double act. 'But you have forgotten the Beethoven concerto afterwards. It has to be Graves. Sit down, Philip—allow me to choose the wine. Graves—from the southern part of the region, wouldn't you say, Sasha?'

'Definitely.' How she wished she could quote a couple of Châteaux names. But her fervent response was all Adam needed. He returned to the table with the bottle of wine and four glasses. As he proceeded to pour the wine, she said mischievously, 'What do you suggest for the interval, Adam?'

'That's already taken care of,' he replied without turning a hair, though his expression of saintly musicianship slipped slightly as he handed Sasha her wine. 'It would be sacrilege to take anything but Malvern water.'

Philip spluttered into his Graves. 'Malvern water? I'm paying, you know!'

Sasha said quickly, 'Ah, but where else do you get that clean, fresh, pure sensation?'

And it was Rachel who answered, 'From Britten's music, of course.'

Adam said, 'So you agree with me? I'm so glad about that.'

Rachel said, 'It isn't difficult. There's no fresher, purer modern composer, is there, Philip?' And Philip, after a sidelong look at Sasha, who was nodding vigorously, so that the glasses slipped down her nose, was able to agree whole-heartedly.

There was no doubt that Rachel was comely. She had a perfect complexion, bright, intelligent dark eyes, and a slim, vibrant figure, which was probably what had attracted Philip in the first place. Sasha decided that they were well-suited, once Philip had stopped being frightened of his girlfriend's keenness about music. She looked at Adam, and saw the same idea in his mind also. They exchanged a conspiratorial smile.

CHAPTER TEN

THE four concert-goers joined the throng in the foyer of the Philharmonic Hall. Adam led the way, because it was his box they were using, and he was familiar with the place. Sasha decided that Philip looked less than happy at being surrounded by musical people, and she positioned herself next to Rachel, with the intention of putting in a good word for Philip. He was wearing his best suit and his hair was tidy—unusual for him, as he was always more dashing in casual clothes, his Porsche keys dangling in his hand, and his hair fashionably unkempt. Sasha felt for him, because she recognised genuine love in his eyes when he looked at Rachel, and Sasha had learnt, to her own cost, what being in love was all about.

They found the box and seated themselves rather self-consciously. It was Rachel who said, 'I come here so often, but never sit in such a distinguished place—a box is something special.'

Adam said quickly, 'I plead not guilty for having it—it was a gift from one of my grateful patients.'

Sasha decided it was a good time to put a word in for Philip. 'But how many concerts do you miss because of work, Adam?'

He smiled, recognising her drift. 'Most.'

Sasha turned to Rachel. Smiling, she said, 'You must appreciate that in our job we are either working or studying. I must say, I'm very much missing out on culture. Even consultants have so much reading it doesn't leave much time for doing what you really would like to do. Leisure is a word that doesn't figure in medical dictionaries.'

She could see Philip putting on a martyred look; she

had chosen the right approach. If only her glasses weren't so uncomfortable. She had done her bit for Philip, and she hoped he was grateful! He coughed, slightly embarrassed, then said bluntly, 'To be absolutely honest, I don't know anything about this Benjamin Britten.'

There was a hush between them, during which the hubbub of the audience and the tuning up of the orchestra filled their ears. Then Rachel said sweetly, 'Then we must start with the Spring Symphony. You'll enjoy that. Then, darling, I'll give you some private tuition.'

Philip said, keeping his face straight, 'I'll enjoy that.' And Rachel giggled first, before Adam and Sasha had time to laugh. An atmosphere of togetherness had been struck, which lasted the whole evening.

In the interval, Adam, true to his word, had laid on a tray of four glasses and a bottle of Malvern water. Sasha smiled as it was brought to them, but Adam hissed in her ear, 'He's driving that Porsche! Never mind Britten—he's got to be sober, or I wouldn't let him drive.'

She looked up at Adam, amused. 'You're really very clever, Adam.'

He smiled at her. 'I don't want any harm to come to my friends.' And his voice was so sweet and gentle that she found herself hoping against hope that he included her in that category.

As they went back to their seats Philip was at the front of the box, with Rachel between him and the other two. Adam whispered, 'This is OK, except that we can't reach Philip to prod him awake when he falls asleep after all that Graves.'

The lights dimmed, and Sasha gladly took off her glasses. 'Don't worry. I'll tell Rachel that he was up all night saving lives.'

'Good thinking.' Adam leaned back in his seat. Then he tapped her arm just as the conductor came on stage, and said quietly during the applause, 'Dr Norton, I see you have depths of wickedness.'

'For a good cause!' she whispered back.

'I agree. They make a good couple. Let's hope it succeeds.' And they sat back as the music started. Philip didn't fall asleep. And afterwards he asked Rachel some questions. Adam and Sasha exchanged another secret look. Their mission of match-making seemed to have succeeded.

After the concert Adam was tactful. 'I'll run Sasha back to the hospital.'

Philip said, 'Not at all—she's my guest.'

Adam said, 'Actually, I would welcome the trip—I'd like to take a look at the child I operated on this morning.'

Rachel held out her hand. 'It was such a pleasure to meet you both.'

Adam said generously, 'My box is yours when you want it.'

'You mean that?' For a moment they forgot she was arty and a bit intense, and saw only a girl given her heart's desire.

'I do mean it. Don't hesitate to ring me.'

They walked to Adam's Rover. Sasha said, 'You really are a kind person, you know.'

He opened the door for her. 'It's nice to be in a position to do it.' He sat down and started the car. As he fastened his seat-belt, he imitated Sasha's voice—'"I always find Chablis just right before Rossini."'

'Don't mock! We did Philip a good turn tonight.'

'Who's mocking? We did them both a good turn, I'm sure. They're good for each other—didn't you think so?' And suddenly he leaned over and kissed the tip of her nose. 'You're lovely,' he said, and indicated right as he nosed the Rover out of the car park. 'Why have I never seen this side of you before?'

'It doesn't surface very often.'

'It's a whole lot of fun, though.'

Sasha looked across at his profile. Poor man—his life hadn't been a lot of fun. Not since Deborah had first become ill, probably. And tonight there was a lift to his lips, and a light in his eye, and she knew it wasn't all because of the music.

He drove almost to the porch of the residence, then turned off the engine. And she knew that she couldn't invite him in, because she was Joe's girl. Suddenly she was conscious of the coldness of the night, the frost in the air. He turned and said, 'Goodnight, then, partner.'

She smiled. 'Goodnight.' She reached for the door-handle, but his arm had reached across and found it for her. And his face was just beside hers. There was no way they could avoid a kiss, and it turned into a longer and more intense one than she had intended . . . Her voice was suddenly husky as she thanked him for bringing her back. But two nurses appeared round the side of the building, and Sasha quickly got out of the car, fearing yet more unfounded gossip. She ran upstairs, then sat by her electric fire for a while, going over the evening in her mind. She had thought she knew Adam Harrington pretty well—yet tonight he had shown that, in spite of his unhappy life, his sense of humour had not been lost. She undressed slowly, reflecting that she and Adam might have helped the other couple towards a happy life together —while she and Adam could never be more than they were this evening.

When sleep didn't come she sat up and read a couple of medical journals that she hadn't had time to open. She read them through right to the advertisements at the end—and there she saw something that seemed, at that late hour of the night, to be a beacon beckoning her onward. It was an advertisement of a surgical job in Chester. Nothing remarkable, except that she had never really bothered to think about opportunities in other regions. But, the more she read through the requirements, the more she thought she might have a chance. And by moving away from Liverpool she would avoid the necessity of being too close to Joe. More than that, she wouldn't always be running into Adam Harrington, who always seemed to turn up just when she thought she had got him out of her system.

She spoke to Joe about it the next time she visited him in his newly decorated flat. He said quietly, 'Seems like a nice job. You want to get away from here, then?'

'Not too far, Joe. Chester is near enough to visit. In two years I'll be better qualified to apply to come back to a teaching hospital in Liverpool. I'll see you at weekends.'

Joe said, his blue eyes wise and sensible, just as they used to be, 'You have to think of your career, love. If this will help, then Godspeed. And you mustn't worry about me. I'm back to coaching at the club. It won't be long till I'm back to normal.'

'That's marvellous.'

'It's fine—I'm OK so long as I don't want to go anywhere—like Chester, for example.' He smiled, but she knew he felt already how far they would be parted.

'Tell you what, Joe—why don't I buy a car? I can get a bank loan. You come with me to choose one next Saturday—and then, even if I do go away, we know we can always be sure of getting together when we want to.'

'You sure you want me to come?'

'I certainly do! I don't know the first thing about cars—and anyway, we'll be going out for trips—to the Lake District, or to Dovedale. You won't feel so shut in any more.'

'That's good of you, lass. I do feel these four walls a bit close sometimes.'

Sasha said, her mind running away with her, 'We both feel that, Joe. Don't you see? We both need to enlarge our horizons a bit. Chester is the answer. The job won't be vacant for months, but I can always write for a form. Thanks for letting me talk it over with you, Joe. You've always been there when I've needed someone to listen—and you've never let me down.'

'I hope that's the way it will always be, love.' He pulled her into his arms, and hugged her. He looked at her with a strange light in his eyes, and Sasha found she couldn't meet the deep affection in them, and turned away.

Joe had promised to take the two girls out to town for a meal. Barbie insisted that they accept, because it would be his first trip to town after his hospital admission. Now that Sasha intended to buy a car, and made a point of seeing her bank manager about a loan, they decided to unite the two trips and make a day of it. But, because Joe's hair was still almost non-existent, on the first Saturday they settled for a meal at Joe's instead, and the girls bought food and a bottle of wine and took them round.

Joe welcomed them. Barbie said, 'I know you didn't want fish and chips, so here's some health foods!' And she spilled a bundle of fruit and vegetarian rissoles and bhajis. Sasha realised then that Barbie had visited a whole lot more than she had. Sasha didn't know anything about Joe's latest food fads and his interest in healthy eating.

Sasha said glumly, 'I'm sorry, Joe—I couldn't get any vegetarian wine.' She produced her bottle of sparkling wine. 'I suppose you prefer Perrier, do you? Or herbal tea?'

But Joe took the bottle with a grin. 'We don't carry these fancies that far,' he said, going in search of an opener.

But Sasha watched them that evening, saw that they had more to talk about, more experiences to share, than she had. It hadn't occurred to her quite so starkly before that Joe might get to a stage of not needing her quite so much. She waited until after ten that night—but as the others were still chatting and playing records she excused herself, pleading tiredness. Barbie laughed. 'Just like in Zaramos!' she said. 'Couldn't keep up with me, could you, Sasha?'

'I'm just more of a lark than an owl, I suppose.'

Barbie didn't offer to walk back with her, but stayed on with Joe, and she heard their laughter as she walked down the little path and opened the squeaky metal gate. She walked back along the row of Victorian houses, with their tiny gardens and overgrown hedges. The moon shone brightly; suddenly she didn't feel cold, and realised that spring was coming. Spring—and with it, a whole new challenge for her if she wanted to take it, a new life in a new hospital. She could forget Adam in peace—and perhaps see Joe less, if he appeared not to need her so much. She straightened her back as she walked, feeling the sap of youth rising in her, the hope and optimism that life would perhaps bring her through today's difficulties.

As she crossed the car park, there was a group of nurses coming home. She didn't mean to listen, but when she heard her own name she turned her head to catch what was being said. In the midst of other chatter, one was saying, 'She's not Harrington's type, surely?'

'If you say so. But they were in his car and they were kissing.'

'Poor thing—he'll eat her alive. She'll turn into another Sister Pearce.'

'Don't say that. That was a terrible thing.'

'Well, he's got those kind of eyes, I always say. Not his fault, I suppose.'

Sasha went to bed extremely mystified. Who could she ask about this Sister Pearce? She recalled that Adam had said something about one of the sisters in his department suffering from depression. Would that be Pearce? And would her depression have been caused by being hopelessly besotted by her handsome chief consultant? It did seem likely. Sasha smiled to herself. Yet another good reason for getting out of Liverpool. It seemed like a good idea to get out now, before it was too late. She settled down in bed, pulled the lamp closer, and opened her Cunningham's Anatomy Manual. There was still the small matter of an exam to pass.

On Friday in Casualty, Philip Mortimer was in an extremely good mood. 'Party tonight in the mess. All invited, and I don't want anyone backing out—it's my engagement.'

So Rachel had confirmed the relationship. Sasha was delighted, and said so. Philip said, 'You helped. You helped a lot.'

'Good—I've never been an agony aunt before. Do you think the glasses helped?'

'Hardly! But *you* did, so I expect to see you there.'

'I'll look in, of course. But I must do some studying first.'

She went down late. She hadn't invited Joe, but when she walked in he was standing in a corner with a group of his friends. He was wearing a striped woolly hat, which he constantly had to remove to show people his scar. She went up to him. 'Joe, you're looking great.'

He smiled, unperturbed that she hadn't invited him. 'Hi, Sasha—you got here just in time. The good champagne's almost finished. Philip is getting out the Californian next.'

Barbie came up. 'Come on, everyone—someone's going to propose a toast. Here, I've got some wine. Anyone not got a glass? Oh, Sasha, glad you could make it. Here, take mine!'

One of the registrars stood on a chair and told everyone what they already knew, that Philip had successfully eluded matrimony for many years in favour of his Porsche—but now it was the only thing on his mind, since he had met the lovely Rachel. There were cheers for the couple, and then Philip stood up, his arm around Rachel. Everyone went quiet for the second time as he spoke quietly, and for once sincerely.

'I can honestly say I've never been one for the flowers and moonlight stuff. But you know, you guys out there—there's a lot to be said for it. I recommend it to all single people. Now, who can I see looking a bit peaky? Ah—Chris Low—now who can we find for you?' There was a chorus of boos and suggestions. Then Phil pointed to Sasha. 'And Sasha, my lovely SHO—you have a sad look around the eyes. Take my tip, Sasha, and settle down!'

Sasha slipped out of the limelight as soon as she could, but Rachel Routledge found her. 'I wanted to thank you again for the other night. You were so nice and funny—you and Adam—I really felt at home with you. I haven't enjoyed a concert so much for ages. We must do it again.' So Rachel wasn't as blind to their little subterfuge as they had thought.

'I'm so very happy for you.'

'You haven't seen Adam? He did promise to look in.' Sasha's heart contracted. She didn't want to see him, not now she had decided to make the break. But if he walked in she must just make the best of it. Thank goodness he wasn't there when Philip was making jokes about her.

She decided to call it a day. Saying goodnight quietly to Barbie and Joe, she explained that she had some more work to do. Joe said, 'I'll see you across the flags, love. I know there's no prowler now—but better safe than sorry.'

They walked over, his arm loosely round her shoulders. She shivered a little in the sudden coolness. He hugged her to him. She said, 'I'm sorry I didn't invite you myself, Joe——'

'Come on, Sasha—you've got enough on your plate just now. Think about that exam and nothing else for a while, OK?'

'You're smashing, Joe.' She put her arms round his neck and pulled him down for a kiss. 'Goodnight. Thanks for seeing me home.' He hugged her again, and sent her up quickly before she caught cold. She waved from the window, and then drew her curtains and changed into her nightshirt and sheepskin slippers to snuggle in the corner of the sofa to read some more. But before she found her place the doorbell rang. She went to the hall.

'Who is it?'

'Adam.' She ran to the door. He shouldn't have come, but she knew she had secretly hoped he would.

She unbolted the front door. Adam stood outside, a fashion-plate in evening dress and black tie. She stared. 'What is it?'

He smiled. 'How come some women look ravishing in nightgown and slippers?' And her heart beat fast as she anticipated his closeness.

'Come in.' It wouldn't do if anyone heard that. The nurses downstairs already missed nothing. 'It must be important. Do you know what time it is?'

'Yes—after midnight, but I saw you coming back, so I knew you wouldn't be asleep.' He stood in the doorway. She gestured to a chair, hastily removing her coloured pictures of the blood vessels supplying the liver and pancreas. 'I'm actually on my way in—emergency craniotomy. As you see, I don't usually dress like this for theatre—I was entertaining friends. I wondered if you'd care to assist? My registrar is at the party—and it might help you with your exams.'

He had seen her come back with Joe, then. Seen them kiss—oh, well, that would show him that she was independent from his advice. 'Assist? Me? I'd—love that, but . . .' so it was nothing to do with her fatal attraction!

'Just fling on something warm and come over.'

'A road accident, is it?'

'Found unconscious in Chinatown. Could be anything.'

'Thanks for thinking of me.' She ran to the bedroom, and pulled on jeans and a sweater. 'Ready!' She was embarrassed at herself for even thinking that Adam would have anything else but work on his mind.

'Sure I'm not pressuring you? You can say no if you're tired.'

She paused at his side, looked into those familiar grey eyes. 'I know that.' Her voice was quiet with the

triumph of knowing that soon she would be far away in
Chester, where his magic couldn't get to her. 'I want to
come very much. I want to pass my exam.'

'Then let's go.'

They strode across the car park, Sasha trying to keep
in step with her longer-legged companion. He told her
briefly what he knew about the patient. They walked to
the lift. Somehow, being inside that square space
together made Sasha suddenly embarrassed. Adam
regarded her gravely as they swished up to the operating
theatres. Just as they were ready to step out, he said
quietly, 'Remember?'

It was a blow under the belt. There she was,
confident, sure of her commitment to Chester, to her
own future—and Adam, in one word, rugby-tackled her
determination. As they walked together towards the
operating-suite, looking to any onlooker like a couple of
cool, efficient surgeons, Sasha's heart was thudding
against her ribs as memory after memory of that
moonlit, lavender-scented island flooded into her
conscious mind from the deep cellars of her
subconscious, memory after memory of that night when
she had learned how to be a woman. It was fortunate
that they were led quickly to the patient, lying in deep
coma in the ante-room. The young houseman, earnest
and worried in his clean white coat and steel-rimmed
glasses, looked visibly relieved to see Adam.

'Gang warfare?' asked Adam, seeing that the victim
was Chinese.

'No one knows, sir. He was brought in unconscious,
bleeding from the ear. I've examined him, sir, but
there's nothing to find except a scalp abrasion—
might have done it falling down—and a bit of neck
rigidity.'

Adam turned to Sasha. 'What do you think?'

'Coma—surely there isn't much chance . . .?'

Adam nodded. 'His chances are minimal. Let's get
scrubbed.' And he had thrown his jacket aside,
expensive though it was, and had his arms up to the

elbows in hot water, before Sasha had time to take off her sweater.

No one spoke as Mr Chan was wheeled in. Adam incised the skin in total silence, and then the whine of the saw filled the night air, high and piercing. 'Sister, swabs and cautery ready, please.' A burst of fresh blood followed the plate of bone, and Sasha used the suction pump to keep the area clear for Adam to look for the source of the bleeding. 'He hasn't a lot of chance of being normal after this, poor fellow.' But Adam worked intensely. 'Let's give him a life if we can.' He found the affected artery. 'Microscope, Sister.' He moved his position as the rest of the operation was carried out microscopically. 'Right, I've trimmed the artery—now it has to be anastomosed.' He was speaking for the benefit of his houseman and Sasha, and they stared, fascinated, as Adam's fingers performed miracles with tiny blood-vessels and even tinier needles. 'We'll take our time. No point in bungling the job.'

Sasha's back was aching before Adam showed any sign of discomfort. At one point he demanded an artificial dacron tube to reinforce his repair. Then he leaned back, stretched his arms, and said, 'Right. Let's get the skin back. I'll leave the bone out in case we have to go in again.' He beckoned to Sasha to come round to his side of the table, and she found herself with the needle, suturing the scalp wound. She did it, without hurry, as he had indicated, but efficiently and without fuss.

As she tied the final stitch, the houseman said, 'That was terrific, Sasha.'

Adam said, 'Not bad. You'll make a surgeon.' And he directed the insertion of the drainage tube and drip. He turned away as the patient was taken to Recovery. 'There was no leakage from that repair. If he's said his prayers tonight, he'll come back to us.'

Sasha sat down on a hard wooden chair. She said tiredly, 'I'll never, ever be able to do that.'

'Me neither.' The houseman sat next to her.

Adam smiled as he stripped off his gown, cap and mask. 'It's all confidence. When you know you are his only chance, you do it, believe me.'

Sister called from the corridor, 'Coffee in here, Doctors.'

Sasha followed the houseman, while Adam went to get changed first. As they drank well-earned coffee, the houseman said, 'I say, when you pass your exams next month, would you be willing to sell me some of your books?'

'You bet. Anyone who says "when" instead of "if" is my friend.' She smiled at him, suddenly feeling older, more experienced. She had just assisted the top neurosurgeon—and done herself credit, too. It was a nice, warm feeling, not entirely due to the temperature of the coffee. She decided it was time to go—yet Adam hadn't appeared. She had done her bit for him. No need to talk about it any more. She tapped at his room door, and peeped in. Adam sat in his chair with his black tie in his hand, his arms sprawled on the desk and his head on his arms. He was fast asleep.

Sister came up behind her. 'I'll wake him later. Let him rest just now. He's been on the go for hours. And he has important guests staying with him.'

'More professors?'

'Might be. He said friends from Greece. He hasn't brought them in to the department.'

Sasha walked to the lift along the silent corridor. She was sleepy after the effort she had put into the operating. But she was bowled over by the news the sister had just given her. Visitors from Greece meant Zaramos, surely? Zaramos meant Artemis . . .

The lift arrived. As she went down alone, she smiled wryly at Adam's remark earlier. 'Remember?' She was remembering all right. She would never forget that magic night. But, somehow, the image of the glossy-haired Greek beauty blotted out all her happy memories. She dragged her feet as she left the lift. Then she opened her eyes very wide. 'Joe!'

'Thought you might be glad of a cocoa.' He put his arm round her and they walked outside together. Behind them, the lone figure of Adam Harrington walked wearily to his car.

CHAPTER ELEVEN

ADAM had lifted a hand in tired farewell as he passed them, but there was something in his face that said he didn't want to talk. Joe's grip tightened. His voice was gruff as he said, 'Adam Harrington's still pretty important to you, huh?'

'A bit.' Sasha was too weary to pretend.

'Only a bit? That's not what I heard. Let's face it—he was here when I was in the ward. It's common knowledge. Everyone knows he fancies you like crazy.' He let go of her suddenly and turned away. 'Lord knows I've no right to speak, after the way I treated you. I know most of it is gossip around this place, Sasha, love—but I also recognise the truth, and I think we should be straight with each other.'

She didn't answer. They went upstairs, into the flat, and he put the kettle on while she drew the curtains. She came back to see him sitting on the sofa, his woolly hat being twisted in his hands. Her heart was sad at the angle of his head, the miserable eyes. She said, 'Thank you for being honest, Joe.'

He looked up. There was a hint of hope in his voice as he said, 'Will you be honest, too? Can you tell me the truth?'

She knelt at his feet, looked up into his eyes. She couldn't tell him the truth, that she adored Adam Harrington with all her heart and soul. How could she say that to Joe? 'I will—I promise—when I know it myself.'

He stood up. 'You still coming to buy a car on Saturday?'

'Yes, I certainly am.' She scrambled to her feet too. 'And Joe—there really is nothing between Adam and me.'

The kettle boiled, but neither of them took any notice. Joe said, 'I trust you, then. I believe you. But I think Adam wants you. I know it.'

She said, trying not to grit her teeth, 'But do I want him?'

Joe sighed. 'I don't know that yet.' Then he tried to smile. 'But you're a great kid, and I'll be here on the dot on Saturday.'

'That's what I wanted to hear.' But as she waved to him from the window she knew she couldn't go on for much longer. Adam had been right—it was pointless trying to be a Girl Guide where feelings were concerned. It wasn't fair to either of them. Glad that she was so weary, she flopped into bed and slept almost at once.

Sasha was glad that Barbie was coming along for the day in town. The three of them went to the garage, and, as Joe was the only one with any knowledge of the internal combustion engine, the girls stood by while he negotiated a fair price for a second-hand black Metro MG. The smooth salesman was impressed by Sasha's status. 'If you'll come this way, Doctor, you can let us know how you want to pay.'

Barbie insisted on the Orchard Tea Rooms for lunch, where the girls had enjoyed baked potatoes that cold November day when they had been shopping for clothes for Zaramos. 'I just adore baked potatoes,' smiled Barbie, looking at Joe with a shake of her head. 'What a pity you're on a diet.'

'Baked potatoes are on my diet,' he assured her gravely. 'The bigger the better, and with lots of butter!' For a moment Sasha felt left out of their banter. It would be nice if Barb and Joe . . .

'What—or who—are you thinking of so deeply, Sasha?' demanded Barbie.

She blushed a little, but said openly, 'Chester. I've written about a job there, and they seem interested.' As her friends stared, she went on, 'Chester isn't Australia, for goodness' sake!' And, though they insisted they would miss her, Sasha again felt slightly redundant, as the other two showed no signs of being lost without her.

They walked slowly down to the Albert Dock after lunch. There were the usual actors dressed up as hurdy-gurdy men with stuffed monkeys, as old-fashioned dockers with mufflers and string round their trousers, as market 'Mary-Ellens' with aprons and shawls, as workhouse children, except they sang Beatle songs, and 'The Leaving of Liverpool'. Joe said suddenly, 'Hey, how about this?' And he indicated a brass plate at the smart door of one building that read 'A T Harrington FRCS'. Sasha felt that familiar twist in her heart. Thank goodness she would be leaving for Chester, and wouldn't have to be reminded of Adam Harrington so often, see him almost daily, and remember his gentleness, his closeness, his sensitive expert kisses . . . Joe went on, without looking at Sasha, 'He must have gone private.'

Barbie did look at Sasha. 'Did you know he worked here?'

Sasha shook her head. 'But he lives here.' And, as they were both looking at her, she had to admit that she knew. Nodding towards the luxury flats, she said, 'Over there. The penthouse, I think.'

'Penthouse! Have you been? And not told us?'

Sasha was able to smile and tell the truth. 'No, never. We aren't all that friendly, you know.' And as she looked back at that neat brass plate she was glad that, in spite of her desperate and hopeless love, she could also think that she, too, would one day put FRCS after her name, even if perhaps she never made quite such a superb surgeon as Adam.

A rowing-boat was offering round trips of the docks for a couple of pounds. Barbie wanted to go, so Joe offered to take them. Sasha shook her head. 'I'll watch.' And she leaned on the railings. 'Go on! I won't criticise your technique!'

Barbie went on to buy the ticket. Before he followed her, Joe paused and looked into Sasha's eyes. 'You said you'd tell me when you knew.'

Barbie was waving the ticket. Sasha said quickly,

nervously, 'Oh, Joe—he isn't even thinking of me in that way, but—I can't get him out of my head. I'm afraid it won't be easy.'

'I think I knew. But when I saw your face—just looking at the bloke's name on a brass plate! Sasha, love—don't wait for us. I know you don't want to.'

For a long moment they looked into each other's eyes. 'Now you know why I'm going away?' she asked.

'Yes,' Joe said. Barbie was waving, and he turned to follow her.

As he turned back, Sasha said, 'Go. And be happy.' Her eyes stung with tears. She said hopelessly, 'I didn't want to say anything, Joe—you made me. I wanted to wait till the infatuation wore off . . .'

Joe came back and suddenly caught her into his arms. 'I wouldn't want it that way, love, and you know it.' And with a final hug he left her and ran down the stone steps to the waiting boat. Barbie waved again, not realising what had gone on. Sasha turned away. Joe would tell her—in good time.

She watched them through eyes misted with tears until they had rounded the small square dock and were out of sight. Then she took a deep breath, pushed her shoulder-bag up, wiped her eyes and set off towards the exit.

There was a small hold-up at the gates. Saturdays were always busy at the docks, and Sasha waited, not caring who was in front of her. But then she caught snippets of conversation.

'Bloody 'ell, Mury—if she isn' a film star, I don'no oo is!'

'How about that silver fox fur, then!'

'I bet that's 'er Rolls!'

Curiosity struggled through Sasha's misery, and she looked between heads at the vision they were staring at. Then she caught at her throat with a stifled gasp. It was Artemis Daniacos. She was being driven by a chauffeur in a black Rolls Royce, and she was waving through the open window at Adam Harrington, before the lights changed to green and the Rolls glided away.

The jam of people lessened, then, and Sasha joined the stream going out through the great stone archway. Suddenly she felt her hand caught by another hand, and she was pulled gently but firmly backwards. She didn't have to look to know who her captor was. 'Adam, let me go—please?'

He looked down into her face, and her resolve melted. Adam said, 'I always hoped I could show you my flat. Are you really in such a rush?'

'I'm not in a rush.'

'Then?'

How could she say that she didn't want to come to an apartment where Adam and Artemis had just made love? She had no proof, of course, but it was highly probable. He was cruel and insensitive to ask her. Then she paused. Didn't she believe that Adam Harrington was sensitive? He had never hurt her knowingly, as a surgeon, as a lover . . . The magnetism that had drawn them together that first stormy night, when, in spite of the rain and the cold, neither had wanted to be the first to say goodnight . . . 'Just for a moment, then.'

'I'm glad.' He didn't speak again as they made their way back across the cobbled pathways towards the block of flats that was part of the renovated docks. But he stayed close—without touching her, his arm was always just behind her, protecting her and guiding her in the crush of humanity all around them. And even that closeness made her sad. Where else in the world would she ever find such a man? Yet as they reached the entrance, Sasha began to feel sick. She knew it would hurt her, seeing how he lived and knowing that she could never be part of his life. She knew she would lie in bed tonight and weep because she had been given a glimpse of the promised land that she knew could never be hers.

In the lift, she was praying that he wouldn't say anything. It was such a small space—he would read her emotions too easily. But he said nothing, merely waiting until they reached the top floor, and then ushering her before h¡m towards a modern, yet classic, wooden door. The brass plate was there again, with the addition 'Residence'. As he took out his key, Adam said quietly, 'So you are allowed time off for good behaviour?'

She turned, stung into a retort. 'Joe isn't like that! Anyway—how did you know?'

'I was watching.' Adam took her coat and hung it in a cloakroom. The carpets were thick, a delicate pale blue, and the air of luxury clung to every curtain, every blind, every rosewood occasional table. Out of the window the view of the estuary, deep blue and beautiful past the Liver Buildings, was breathtaking. It was getting dark now, and some lights were on in boats on the river, and in buildings on the other side, in Cheshire. Adam went on, 'You're still involved, then?'

Sasha tried to think of something clever to say. 'Joe is always there when you need him.'

He said quietly, 'Yeah. After a couple of kids you won't even remember there might be anything else.'

She had to turn and face him then. 'If you mean that being with Joe means being a housewife and not a surgeon, then you're wrong, Mr Harrington!'

Adam crossed the room to put some small onyx table-lamps on. On a side table was a silvery pail with an unopened bottle of champagne sticking out. 'Mr Harrington, eh? I must have said something wrong.'

'Just a little.' Her voice was hard.

Adam came up suddenly. 'Sasha, I'm so sorry. The exam is coming up, and I didn't want to fight with you—only wish you well. Will you let me?' He was standing very close, and she felt her hunger for him steal over her like a gossamer spell. She tried not to turn towards him, but her body beat her determination and in a moment she was in his arms, holding him as tightly as he held her.

He didn't open the champagne until after a long and impassioned embrace. But through her bliss and her enchantment came the memory of the beautiful

Artemis, and Sasha fought her longings, steeled herself
against the kisses of the man she loved but knew she
could never have. She walked shakily to the window,
heard the pop of the champagne cork. She said without
turning, 'Isn't it a bit soon for celebration?'

Adam brought her a cool crystal glass, the bubbles
winking and sparkling. 'I know you'll do it.' He raised
his glass in a silent toast and she touched hers briefly
against his. As they drank he moved closer. Then he took
her glass from her, their bodies touching, his hardness
thrusting against her. 'You will let me know—when you
get back from Glasgow? Or will it be Joe?'

Softly, breathlessly, she had to speak the truth. As
he held her without pressure, their faces close but
not touching, she said, 'Joe and I have—let each other
go.'

He let out a long breath. 'Well done, my dear.'

'Why?'

He took her shoulders so that he could look deep into
her eyes, and she fell in love with his grey gaze yet again.
'Because it wasn't right. Because, for all your goody-
goody idealism, you would have driven each other to
screaming pitch within a few months! Because——' And
suddenly he let her go, and sat down on his long settee
and put his head in his hands.

She looked at him in consternation. Perhaps he did
care for her, yet was regretting that Artemis had a prior
claim on him. Sasha said hastily, 'I'd better go, I think.'

'Why? Why?' He looked up. 'Do you want to?'

She went to the window. It was almost dark now, and
the lights from the ships were lovely, like fairyland, and
the floodlit buildings made Liverpool very beautiful.
'I'll miss this place. Liverpool isn't bad, you know.'

He was by her side at once. 'You're leaving?'

She sensed his disapproval, his annoyance. But she
knew it was pointless ever hoping to be part of this
wealthy, glamorous life that Adam shared with Artemis
and her brother, the life of the millionaire's yacht, the
Greek islands. Sasha was from a small stone cottage in

the Pennines. And although one day she would be a surgeon—and with luck a good one—this sort of background was not for her. Artemis belonged, and Artemis would be the one to replace Deborah in Adam's lonely heart.

She said, 'I'm going to Chester Infirmary in August.'

There was a silence. A ferry, lit up from stem to stern, rode in like a stately empress on the evening tide. Adam said harshly, 'You didn't think of discussing this with your colleagues?'

She said quietly, 'Do you mean with you?'

'As I had already offered you a job, yes, I do. I think you should have asked my opinion of Chester. I might have—been able to suggest a better place to train.' He walked away suddenly, strode up and down the room, before picking up his champagne glass and draining it.

Sasha took her own glass, not knowing what to say. As she sipped, she stared out at a flashing red light. Two short flashes, then a break before two more. Pilots must have used those lights decades ago, when the great transatlantic liners used the channels. Now, of course, everyone used planes. And some their private jets . . . She said, 'So Artemis is going home? I hope she enjoyed her visit to Liverpool.'

His voice was strangled. He said, 'She isn't going yet. She's staying the night with friends, then going on to New York. I—I'll be flying out with them, I expect. They have been trying to persuade me.'

Sasha turned to face him. 'So it's goodbye, then?'

Adam came towards her. 'Shall we say "*au revoir*"?'

'Well—yes . . .'

'After all—you might still want to work for me after a couple of years in Chester?'

She managed a smile. 'I think I would, to be honest. You are the best surgeon I've ever—watched.' She wanted to say 'loved', but realised she had never been in love before, so there was no one to compare Adam with. She said, 'I think I'd better be going.'

'I'll drive you home.'

'No—please, no!'

Adam said acidly, 'I haven't got a contagious disease. There's no need to make it quite so obvious that you don't want me around.'

Sasha's resolve crumpled. 'Oh, Adam—please don't. You don't know how miserable I am at this moment, you really can have no idea——' But she could say no more as her mouth was crushed by his, and the breath almost squeezed from her body. He carried her into the bedroom, where he laid her gently on the satin quilt. Neither of them spoke as he slowly lay down beside her and gathered her tremulously into his arms.

She saw it as his way of saying goodbye. His kisses this time were sweeter, more poignant than last time, because they both had tears on their cheeks, and Sasha wasn't sure if they were hers or his. He murmured, 'I didn't know if I would ever kiss you again.'

Though she knew she ought to be pushing him away, her body's yearning made her draw his face down to hers, and kiss him first with as much sensuality as he had taught her the first time. She heard him moan with a fraught inner joy, before he gently took control, and, stroking her body with hard, expert hands, he held her and took her with a joyful and mutual passion.

It was Adam who broke away. She had no idea of the time, but he was saying, 'My dear, you need your sleep. I only meant to wish you luck in your exam. Please forgive me for being so selfish, for wanting to keep you here.' He cupped her face in his warm hands, and they looked into one another's eyes. 'Can I make you something to eat? There are steaks in the fridge. Or a sandwich . . .?'

She shook her head. 'I'll just go.'

'Do you think I'd let you go alone?'

They were both silent as she put her coat on. As they went down in the lift he put his arm about her and held her close. But as he drove the Rover through the dark Toxteth streets towards the Western Hospital a wall seemed to come down between them. He's regretting being so nice to me, I expect, she thought. But when he unexpectedly asked her what she was thinking, Sasha said, 'I don't regret anything.' And she heard his sudden intake of breath.

Adam said nothing until they reached the flats. This time there were no nurses to see them as he took her into his arms in one brief last embrace. *'Au revoir*—and good luck,' he whispered.

She said, 'I suppose you have girlfriends in New York?'

Adam looked down at her, smoothed her hair from her eyes with a gentle touch. 'One or two. I won't be lonely.'

She nodded. What else had she hoped he would say? She got out of the car, walked towards her doorway without looking back. But Adam was there, standing, just as he had that night when they had neither of them wanted to say goodnight. He said, 'You'll let me know—about the exam?'

'Oh, yes.'

'How are you getting to Glasgow?'

She smiled a little. 'I bought a car today. I'll be driving myself to Manchester Airport.'

'Businessman's Special, eh?'

'I suppose it must be.'

'You've got a future, Sasha. You really have.'

She said firmly, 'I think so. I just have to prove it to one or two people first!'

The first time they had stood like this, the rain had been beating down. Now, Sasha noticed that the air was kind, and in the light from the porch she could see the buds on the sycamores were bursting, almost opening before her eyes. She looked up at the hospital clock tower. It was almost two in the morning. She reached out her hand and touched Adam's cheek. It was too difficult to say goodbye, so she just said, 'You've helped me—so much.'

He nodded. And in almost total silence he walked back to the open door of the Rover, which was sleek and shining under the light. As he drove away without looking back Sasha breathed in deeply the scent and feeling of spring. In spite of her sadness she had received more than she could describe from Adam Harrington. He had made her a woman, and would make her a surgeon, too. There was no bitterness in her heart, although tonight was the night she had said goodbye to both Joe and Adam. The future belonged to Sasha Norton.

She trod wearily up the stairs. Yet her heart felt suddenly free and uncomplicated. It was right that she should be alone now. She would go ahead, take her exam, take the post in Chester, and treasure her time with Adam deep inside her innermost being, where it would always stay, but soon it would cease to hurt so much. Already she had forgotten his last words to her. But she remembered the tone . . . And she remembered that he had promised he wouldn't be lonely. She hoped so. He had been lonely long enough.

Sasha wasn't on duty the next morning. She spent the time studying, but she noticed Barbie running across to the ward, after hearing her bleep. There was no question now that Barbie would give up. She was well on the way to her goal, and Sasha smiled at the flying white coat and red-gold hair of her friend.

But then she heard the door bang again. She went back to the window, only to see the unmistakable figure of Joe Acourt leaving Barbie's flat with an obviously jaunty step. For a moment she felt a pang of—no—it couldn't be jealousy. Barb and Joe deserved to be happy. And almost as though he heard her words, Joe turned and looked up at the window. Their eyes met. Then she gave him a broad smile and a cheerful wave, a wave he returned with equal vigour. Friends, then—nothing more. And her heart throbbed at that moment for the man who had saved Joe's life. In a moment Joe was gone round the corner of the hospital, and Sasha went back to her books.

There was one further interruption to her work that day. Although it was Sunday, a florist's van drew up outside the residences, and when Sasha's bell rang she opened the door to a huge bouquet of red roses. Heart thumping, she carried them in, and looked feverishly for a message. There was none. So she put them lovingly in a vase, the scent filling the room, and, for the last time, threw herself on the sofa and cried for Adam. She cried until her eyes were red and her chest was sore from the sobbing. But when all her tears were spent she picked up her books, and calmly and silently got on with her life.

He hadn't written 'Goodbye'. But that was what he meant by the flowers. She must look upon him as he did her, as worthy of roses, but, like them, only lasting a few days before withering . . . He would be in New York by now, and Sasha Norton would be a distant memory—one to add to his list, yet not one to regret. Just like Sasha thinking of Adam. A memory never to be forgotten, but never to be regretted either.

The day passed in study, and evening fell. The small flat was filled with fragrance. But Sasha had no more tears, and she felt a great calm steal over her, as though a gentle curtain had been drawn over the recent past, a beautiful play with a bitter-sweet ending.

CHAPTER TWELVE

IT WAS raining in Glasgow. The streets were strange to her, and the atmosphere cold as she took a cab, driven by a very taciturn Scot, to the imposing entrance of the Royal College of Surgeons. It was large and solemn, and it spoke of years of distinguished sons and daughters of Glasgow who had become world-famous surgeons. It also reminded her of saddened students who had failed. But she didn't feel afraid. She entered, neither over-confident nor nervous. She was there to do a job, and the sooner she got on with it, the better.

She sat quietly, not bothering with final revision, as some of those waiting were doing. She had enjoyed the flight from Manchester, only occasionally wondering how it differed from flying to New York on a luxury private jet . . . But she knew that she had made the right decision. She would have despised herself if she had joined the world of people like John Steadman, who was just a social butterfly.

A man walked past who reminded her of an older version of Adam Harrington. 'That's Farley—one of the most famous surgeons in the world,' whispered the boy sitting next to her as they waited. 'Hard to think of him sitting here with his knees knocking, just like us, isn't it?'

'Yes, it is. But famous surgeons are only you and I grown a bit older.'

'That's a good way of looking at it.' He held out his hand. 'Here's hoping we both make it.'

The papers didn't seem all that bad, as she was so familiar now with the questions. They seemed almost like old friends as she went through the multiple choice, finishing before the time allowed, so that she had time to go back and check her answers. She handed her paper in, and was joined by the boy she had spoken to earlier. His name was Ian, and he worked in Walsall. 'Fancy some lunch?'

As they chatted over an onion bridie Liverpool seemed like a distant country. Joe Acourt and Barbie would have gone to visit Chan, who was improving daily. Adam would be leading a life far out of her reach in the bustling streets of New York. But she was here, and she was real, and she was taking the first positive steps on the road to her own life and her own ambition, and it was exhilarating.

The afternoon session went equally well. She was grateful to Adam for finding out for her where she had gone wrong the last time. She was careful to read every word, to understand exactly what the examiners wanted before she made her replies. She went back to the private hotel where many of the entrants were staying, and they ate dinner together before going to their rooms for a final look at slides. Sasha slept well, her mind clear and her emotions under control at last. She was glad she had something as demanding as her exams to take her full attention, and to stop her thinking vainly of things that never could be.

It was raining still when she presented herself at the college the next morning. But there was no gloom in her mind as she recognised the first slide. It was a cirrhotic liver. Then there was a new one, but she had checked it only last night—the HIV virus. The two white-haired gentlemen who asked her clinical questions seemed just like older brothers chatting about interesting cases, or colleagues asking her opinion.

She went with Ian to have a cup of tea. They heard the rush as the list of names went up, but they didn't hurry, knowing that the crowd was too thick to penetrate. When they walked up later her hands were trembling a bit, but she felt almost sure that her name would be there. There was a group of friends who had passed already whooping in the corridor. She stared up at the list. There was no Norton there.

Ian came up. 'Well, we both made it. Congrats, Sasha!'

'But——'

He grinned. 'You can't find it? Look under "With Honours"!'

Her heart thumped as she looked at the small list separate from the main one. 'With Honours in Physiology.' She laughed with the relief of it. 'Wow!' She stood for a moment, until her name became blurred and the tears trickled down her cheeks. And her first thought was of Adam. 'He'll be proud of me.' Then she remembered that he was in America, and had washed his hands of her. Oh, well—she would show him! She would become a surgeon now, maybe one day rival him. She smiled through her tears of joy, and shook Ian's hand hard.

'Let's go and join the gang. They're going in search of Guinness.'

Sasha looked at her watch. 'I think I can just make the six-thirty flight.' They shook hands again, and wished each other luck.

She was still in a rosy glow when she took her seat on the Manchester shuttle. 'Would you like a drink, madam?'

'Yes, please.' And then she realised that when she got off in twenty minutes she would be driving her own car back to Liverpool. 'Ginger ale, please.' And the Scottish steward grinned and said, 'On the wagon, are we?'

She phoned her mother from Manchester. 'I've passed!'

'Wonderful news. Hurdle number one over. We're delighted, darling.'

'One of these days you're going to be proud of me.'

'We already are, you know that. Proud as Punch!'

'See you soon, Mum.' She put the phone back and shivered as a draught whistled through the concourse. There was her shiny little car, waiting patiently for its owner. She unlocked it, flung her bag on the seat, and drove carefully down the ramp and out into a windy, wet night. She turned on the radio as she drove along the motorway, feeling at least three inches taller than when she'd come. She smiled at the traffic that splattered her windscreen with spray. Nobody knew that the little black Metro was being driven by a future surgeon! In fact, from the way a cheeky lorry driver hooted at her, all they saw was an attractive young brunette. Little did they know! She smiled broadly at the driver in his mirror, and he flashed his lights before speeding off in the middle lane.

By the time she reached the M62 she was feeling tired and hungry. But she was still high on her success, and she opened the windows a little to keep herself alert. She turned into the hospital car park at eleven in the evening and all she could think of was a tin of baked beans and a cup of cocoa. She let herself in. The flat looked exactly as she had left it, with unwashed mugs in the sink, and clothes she hadn't needed to pack still strewn over the bed.

The high left her. She was back, she was all alone, and she had a job to do tomorrow. She had no one to talk to tonight, no one to share her achievement with, to bubble over with delight at her pass with Honours. She wondered what Adam was doing at this moment, living the life of the rich and famous. It would have been nice to ring him, to hear his voice lift in pleasure when she told him her news . . . She threw a pair of jeans off the bed and climbed in.

The morning made up for it. All the nurses congratulated her, had known she would do it. Sister McKeown was on this morning, and the news brought brightness to her careworn face. 'I've been saving these,' she said, producing a box of liqueur chocolates. 'I knew you'd do it, love.'

'Thanks, Carrie—but not for me—share them out among everyone.' Philip wasn't on duty, but the rest of the department seemed as pleased as Sasha was.

Barbie came down at lunchtime. Sasha saw her in the distance, and tried to keep her face straight, to pretend that she'd failed. But she couldn't hide the sparkle in her eyes, and Barbie jumped up and down for joy. 'Wonderful, marvellous, fantastic! Does Joe know?'

'Not yet.'

'He's in Nelson Ward—helping Chan with his speech therapy. Why don't you go up? You *are* taking us out to celebrate tonight, aren't you?'

Sasha laughed. 'Of course. I'll take you to the best restaurant in Liverpool.'

'Gosh, you're already talking like a surgeon!' teased Barbie.

One of the porters from the front desk came in just then. 'Dr Norton here? Letter for you, love—left here yesterday, I think.'

Sasha took the white envelope curiously. There was nothing to show where it came from—just her name neatly typed. It must have been handed in. She tore it open—but, when she saw Adam's signature at the bottom, she put it away quickly and said she would read it later. When things had quietened down in Casualty she went into the office for a little privacy while, with shaking fingers, she took out Adam's letter.

'Dear Sasha,' it began baldly, 'I'll be in the States when you get back from Glasgow, but I know you'll pass, and this is to congratulate you and wish you every success in the future.' How distant and polite he sounded. She read on. 'I felt sure we were just beginning to get to know one another. I'm disappointed you'll be moving away from Liverpool—we need conscientious doctors like you around. But I wanted to apologise for being less than gracious to you when I heard. Of course you must go where the good jobs are, and I will always wish you well wherever your work takes you.

'John and Artemis send kindest regards, too. I might be in Tiffany's when you read this—Artemis seems to have set her heart on a diamond or two! Take care, Sasha. God bless you. Adam.'

And then the alert bell sounded, and she stuffed the letter in her white coat pocket and ran towards the entrance, where a coronary case was just being brought in. 'Oh, dear—he doesn't look good. Defibrillator, quick!' She worked heroically to start and regulate his heartbeat. Without fuss she filled a syringe and injected the drug, waited until his eyelids flickered, and then asked him gently where the pain was most severe. She waited until he was more stable, and then sent him up to Chris Low in the coronary unit.

'Doctor? I'm his wife. Is he dead?' asked a small woman with a white, stricken face.

'No, he's not dead, but he has had a heart attack. They'll be looking after him upstairs. Sister will look after you up there.'

'But I heard the ambulanceman say he couldn't feel any pulse. He must be dead, and you won't tell me!'

Sasha put her arm round the little woman's shoulders. 'It's all going to be OK. I got the heart going again. There's every hope, honestly.'

The woman's eyes filled, and she clung to Sasha's hand. 'It's a miracle, it really is. The way you can bring him back.'

'Just modern medicine.'

'Just people like you, you mean. God bless you, love.' She was led away by one of the nurses, still sobbing her gratitude. Sasha looked after them as they walked along the corridor to the lifts, and suddenly felt a tear on her own eyelashes. Starting a heart might be routine to her, but to that little lady it was a miracle. She prayed that her husband would pull through.

Sister McKeown said, 'There's a man dripping blood in Cubicle Two—cut himself on his lawnmower.'

'Lawnmower! Then it really must be spring, and we haven't noticed.' She stitched the cut, which fortunately hadn't gone down as far as the tendons, and gave him an anti-tetanus jab. 'I hope your lawn looks good.'

'Aye, it's grand. My own fault—tried to get the damp grass off the blades without using gloves. It's still wet, you see, the grass. I won't be being clever next time, love. Thanks very much, Doc.'

'You're welcome.'

As the patient left Carrie McKeown came in and said in a low voice, 'There's a man here with a note from his own GP saying that he's got a strangulating testicle.' She handed over the letter. 'But he says he won't see a woman doctor.'

Sasha scanned the letter. 'Well, Phil's off with Rachel to the Lake District for the day, so he can't see to it. Ask Charge Nurse Williams if he'd spare me a few minutes.' She was used to this situation, and Williams was used to standing by and looking important with difficult patients. Together they greeted the man calmly, and emphasised that they couldn't help him unless they examined him. He allowed examination of his painful scrotum, and they admitted him to the surgical ward for emergency operation. Sasha thanked Williams. 'Just think,' she couldn't help saying, 'next year I'll be that surgical registrar coping with the emergency!'

'Sooner you than me, love,' said the taciturn Williams. But he shook her hand all the same, and wished her good luck.

Sasha called, 'Any more?' But the department was quiet for the moment, so Sasha went up to Nelson Ward to tell Joe her news.

'Well done; well done, love!' Joe was with Chan in the single room where he had been himself a short time ago. He gave her a hug and kissed her cheek. 'There was never any real doubt, was there?'

'Thanks. I'll take you out tonight to celebrate.'

'Can't make it tonight. Popular bloke, I am. Some of the girls from my department have booked a table in the new Italian place in Chapel Street. Can we do it at the weekend?'

'Sure.' Sasha felt deflated again. Was there no one she could share her success with? She exchanged a few words with Chan, explaining that she had been there at his operation. She was warmed to see his improvement, since Joe had been giving him intense speech exercises. Perhaps Adam was right never to give up on people.

During the operation she had been sure the unconscious man could never revive—yet here he was sitting up, using his hands, and even smiling in a rather one-sided way.

Joe said proudly, 'When I've finished with him, he'll be doing his kung fu kicks just as high as he used to!'

Chan grinned up sideways. 'If you say so, brother Joe. Brother Joe say something—then OK by me.'

Sasha walked along the corridor. Adam's room was occupied—but only by Pat Moore, who came out just as she passed. 'Hello, Sasha. You made it?'

'Yes, I made it.'

'Knew you would.' Another vigorous handshake. 'Glad you popped up, actually, because Adam left his key for you. He'd like you to keep an eye on the flat for him.'

She stared up in amazement. 'That's extremely rude of him.'

Pat grinned. 'I think he thought you might be at a loose end, now that you aren't studying in the evenings.'

'That's not how I see it,' she said crossly. She took the key from Pat muttering, 'If he thinks I'm trailing down to the Albert Dock just to look at his crummy flat . . .' And she made her way downstairs, the key thrust into the same pocket as the letter. 'What utter cheek!' Fancy him assuming that she was there to run after him while he went off enjoying himself! And buying diamond rings for Artemis, no doubt. Even worse cheek!

But that evening, as she sat alone in the mess, eating leathery lasagne, she began to think that it might pass the time, just to go down and make sure everything was all right. The dock had its own guards, but they couldn't be everywhere—and she wouldn't mind another look around the penthouse. The river would look so lovely by night. And the moon was full tonight. She weighed the key in her hand—then decided. Adam was right, as usual. She was at a loose end, and a drive to the Dock would pass the time.

She walked out into the hospital grounds, conscious of the stars, the opening leaves, and the twittering of sparrows in the shrubbery. The night air was pleasantly warm, the chill of winter past. She swung her car keys, a feeling of pride coming over her as she walked to her own transport. She drove into town telling herself that she was very noble, giving up her valuable time to make sure Adam's place wasn't being vandalised. She parked at the side of the dock. Then she began to feel silly, because there was a perfectly good security man, keys jangling, walkie-talkie radio buzzing, torch at the ready, walking along just in front of her.

She called to him. 'Excuse me, but do you patrol the flats?'

The man turned. 'Sure.' Then he grinned. 'Dr Norton!'

She didn't think she was so well-known. But then she recognised the young black man, immaculate in blue shirt and navy trousers. 'Hey, Gary—that's cool, man!'

He laughed. 'It's a great job, Doctor. But—we usually warn ladies not to walk about alone—even with us here. You never know.'

'I understand. I won't be staying. How's Lily? And your mother?'

'Great, thanks. I'll tell them I saw you.' He suddenly hit his forehead. 'I nearly forgot—I met that consultant friend of yours just a minute ago. If you're meeting him, he's down there by the water.'

'Mr Harrington? No, it won't be him. He's in America.'

Gary scratched his head. 'Must have a double, then.' He wished her goodnight and resumed his patrol, whistle swinging from his belt. Sasha watched him. He couldn't have seen Adam—but how nice if he really were there, and she could talk to him as once they had talked, that fragrant night on Zaramos, telling each other secrets, understanding one another, not noticing the entire night slipping away . . .

She brought herself back to the present. No point in

checking Adam's flat if Gary had just come from there. She would stand for a moment and watch the lights on the opposite shore, and then she would go home. The round lights on their slim black poles looked like giant necklaces as they reached gracefully into the distance towards the floodlit towers of the Liver Building. She leaned on a black-painted bollard, as many a seaman would have done before her, and gazed out to sea.

She was very slowly conscious that someone else had moved up to lean on a neighbouring bollard—someone in an expensive coat and hat—someone who did look extraordinarily like . . . 'Adam!' He was leaning on one elbow, as she had seen him lean on board the *Dolphin*. And his very presence was so dear to her that for a moment she couldn't hide her joy. 'You never went to New York. You were just teasing me—mocking me . . .'

He stood upright as she walked towards him, and lifted his hat courteously. But his eyes showed more than courtesy, as he did his best to hide his pleasure that she had come. 'Only a little, darling.'

'Why didn't you go?'

'I'm not their kind of person. Anyway—you had an exam to pass.'

'But you acted as though you didn't want me around.'

Adam shrugged. 'Was that so wrong? I wanted to find out how you felt about me. Men do foolish things sometimes—am I different from other men?'

She hid a smile. 'But of course—you're a surgeon!'

They both laughed—like old friends, like people who liked each other, who felt at ease together. Then she said, 'It was a bit much, expecting me to run around after you, keeping an eye on your flat!'

'You came, though.' And there was suddenly a catch in his voice as he said, 'Why did you come if you thought it a nuisance?'

She shrugged and turned away, knowing what he wanted her to say, but not playing his game. 'At a loose end, I suppose.'

He said softly, 'No friends, then? No parties?'

She faced him. 'I didn't feel like it.'

'But you felt like thinking of me?'

His look was deep and caring, his voice very low. She didn't even try to pretend then. 'Yes,' she said, 'I did feel like being close to you, even though you have your own charmed circle of friends where I don't fit.'

'Where are they, Sasha?' He held his arms wide. 'See—I'm all alone—just like you.' There was emotion in his voice, and she felt pity for his loneliness, just as she always had.

She turned away and gripped the railing, staring over the black water littered with reflections of the lights over the river. He hadn't gone with Artemis—but where was his memory of Deborah? That still lingered between them, separating them. Adam moved closer, and looked out to where she was looking. 'You still intend to take yourself off to Chester?'

She said, keeping her voice steady, 'Don't talk like the counsel for the prosecution, please.'

'I'm sorry.' He waited for a while, and then said, 'Just one more tiny question. Why did you break with Joe?'

'He didn't need me.'

'But you were determined to be his prop.'

She turned and gave a little laugh. 'You want me to tell you how right you were, don't you? Well, you were—he told me he didn't want me under those conditions.' She looked away again. 'Why did you make such a fuss about it anyway?'

'I didn't want to see your life thrown away.'

'Why?'

'Because I love you, dammit!'

For a moment the world seemed to stop turning. She slowly turned her head and stared at him as he stood, simple, handsome, his grey eyes fixed on her and unaccountably anxious suddenly. Her chin wobbled, and she swallowed hard and tried to take hold of herself and think of something to say. For how many years had this dear, lonely man never said those words to anyone? And now he had said it openly and plainly to her. The shock began to change into a strange, wild, wonderful hope. 'You—you do?'

'I do.'

She said, 'You were always very protective towards me.'

'I've always loved you.'

Suddenly she put both her hands over her face. She had dreamed of him saying that—but now that he had it was more magical than anything she had dreamed. It was real.

She knew he had come closer, because she felt the warmth of his body, felt herself shielded from the gentle sea breeze. He drew her hands away with his. 'Don't be frightened.'

'I'm not. It's just that—I never thought you would love anyone again. Not the way you used to talk of Deborah.'

He nodded, still keeping both hands in his. 'I thought I'd never be whole again when I lost her. But I am, and I know what I'm saying.' He smiled at her. 'Come up to the flat. We can't talk here.'

They walked together, Adam ushering her before him past groups of sightseers around the inner docks. As they neared the flats he put his arm around her, and drew her close against him.

There was a sudden cry. 'Mr Harrington. Mr Harrington!' They stopped and looked back. A woman with a child in a baby buggy was walking towards them. Adam paused and turned. The woman said, 'You remember me, don't you, sir?'

He smiled, and shook her by the hand. 'Sister Pearce. How nice to see you. I hope you're keeping well.'

'Very well, thank you. I—thought you'd like to know—I was married and I've got young Stephanie now. I—er—was a bit of a pest to you once, wasn't I? That's all over. I'm Mrs Hopwood now.'

'I'm glad.'

Sasha didn't say anything. But she was glad to have the mystery of Sister Pearce cleared up happily. The poor lady must have been very much in love at some stage, to suffer from depression. It couldn't have been easy for Adam. He put his arm around her again, and they approached the front entrance to the flats. Sasha took out the key. He said quietly, 'You keep that one.' And Sasha clung to it with a sudden clutching fist. Was he really wanting her to have free entry to his home?

He opened the front door, flung his hat and coat on a chair, and turned to her. He whispered her name. 'Come here—don't leave me.' And she went into his arms, returning his kisses with an open, loving abandon. After a while he led her into the drawing-room, and they sat together on the sofa. He put his arm along the back of the sofa, as he had that night in Zaramos. But tonight he twisted her hair gently in his fingers, played with the lobes of her ears, her cheek and neck, and down to her breasts, his breathing fast and his eyes misty with love. 'Are you afraid?'

She shook her head. 'No.'

'I am.'

'But why?'

'You haven't told me you love me. You haven't said you'll stay with me. If I've got it all wrong, then I don't know what's become of me.'

She smiled. 'You know very well I love you—terribly much. It's just that I've never said it before, that's all.'

He got up suddenly, and walked to the window. 'Does it bother you, that I've been in love before?'

'No, Adam. Truly it doesn't.'

He said, 'But I want you to understand, darling. I have been in love before—deeply. But when I first met you, something hit me that very first day. I felt as though I'd been living in a long night—an arctic night—and that suddenly I could see the dawn.'

'You said that, that night. You said it was like a ray of sun when you'd been expecting rain.'

He smiled. 'You remembered that!'

'I remember everything you've ever said.' She held out her arms. 'Please come back.'

He strode across the room into her arms. As they clung together he said, 'I was madly jealous of everyone you looked after.'

'But who? Patients? You did that, too.'

His smile was warm as he stroked her cheek. 'You are always looking after lame ducks. There was Barbie first. Remember how concerned you were—how you did extra duty for her—and you cooked that delicious meal that I managed to get myself invited to?'

'She was my friend. I had to do something.'

'There was Gary Brooks—how sweet you were to that young man. And there was Joe—always Joe, receiving your full attention, your pity and your concern. Oh, Sasha, it wasn't easy watching all these who seemed more important to you than I was.' She started to tell him that all these had been on the fringes of her concern—that Adam Harrington had been her main preoccupation and obsession since that day he had come down to Casualty, asked her name, cast a spell with those sincere grey eyes. He stopped her. 'Do you remember, I asked you if you knew what I thought of you?'

She laughed. 'I do. Are you going to tell me at last?'

'I was on the point of telling you then how much I loved you. But I held back then—you had enough to do, keeping track of your conscience and Joe Acourt. And you had your books. But, darling—how I wanted you to think of me—look after me as you did everyone else.' He kissed her cheek, lingered over it. 'I was quite simply and childishly jealous. So now you know what sort of fellow I am. I need to be looked after—by you.'

She said softly, 'Will the rest of my life do?'

He held her very close then, and she felt his heart beating against hers. He whispered, 'Will anyone notice if you don't go back tonight?'

'But——' Her mind was in a happy whirl, as she thought of prosaic things like a toothbrush, clean clothes . . . 'No, no one will even think of looking for me.'

He stroked her hair back from her face gently, his surgeon's fingers belonging solely to her at that moment. Then he started undoing the buttons of her blouse. 'Tomorrow,' he said gently, 'I'll go and see about a special licence. And you can start making a wedding guest list. But not now, my Sasha. Now I think we need a little time to ourselves. Will you telephone Chester and tell them you aren't coming, or shall I?'

'I'll do it,' she murmured into his neck, 'in the morning.'

'I can't think why you even applied. Fifty miles away from me! Why?' Her clothes were now in an untidy heap on his Wedgwood blue carpet, and his own were joining them as he kissed her.

She said, 'You know very well. I had to get away from you, because I was hurting too much, seeing you every day and loving you every day, and knowing that you never stayed with anyone for long. I thought if I went away—if I didn't have to be reminded of you so much—that it might help, that if I didn't even see you for two years, the pain might start getting better.'

'Oh, my love.' He gathered her against him, length for length, warm skin against her, arms straining her even closer. 'Has it gone now? You mustn't leave me. Don't ever leave me. I need you so much—more than I've ever needed anyone. I mean it, Sasha. You're my other half, darling, and only when we're together am I complete.'

She lay in his arms that night, her feelings alive, vital, filling her whole body, allowing her to return his passion as she had always wanted to, dreamed of whenever she was with him. And later they slept, his head cradled on her breast. Outside the spring moon glowed white and brilliant. And slowly, silently, the tide turned as they slept, pulsing against the stone walls beneath, lapping with the constancy of eternity.

Hello!

As a reader, you may not have thought about trying to write a book yourself, but if you have, and you have a particular interest in medicine, then now is your chance.

We are specifically looking for new writers to join our established team of authors who write Medical Romances. Guidelines are available for this list, and we would be happy to send them to you.

Please mark the outside of your envelope 'Medical' to help speed our response, and we would be most grateful if you could include a stamped self-addressed envelope, size approximately $9\frac{1}{4}''$ x $4\frac{3}{4}''$, sent to the address below.

We look forward to hearing from you.

Editorial Department,
Mills & Boon Limited,
Eton House,
18-24 Paradise Road,
Richmond, Surrey,
TW9 1SR.

THE IDEAL TONIC

Over the past year, we have listened carefully to readers'
comments, and so, in August, Mills & Boon are launching
a *new look* Doctor-Nurse series – MEDICAL ROMANCES.

There will still be three books every month from a wide
selection of your favourite authors. As a special bonus,
the three books in August will have a special offer price
of **ONLY** 99p each.

So don't miss out on this chance to get a real insight into
the fast-moving and varied world of modern medicine,
which gives such a unique background to drama, emotions
– and romance!

FRUIT SALAD WORDSEARCH
COMPETITION!

How would you like a years supply of Mills & Boon Romances ABSOLUTELY FREE? Well, you can win them! All you have to do is complete the word puzzle below and send it in to us by Dec. 31st. 1989. The first 5 correct entries picked out of the bag after that date will win **a years supply of Mills & Boon Romances** (*ten books every month - **worth £162***) What could be easier?

```
T E T A N A R G E M O P
A N E Y E P A R G A A E
N E A R S P I M N N T A
G N P R T L W E A D Y C
E I R E R E I L R A R H
R R I B A U K O O R R M
I A C P W R C N O I E A
N T O S B A R K E N H N
E C T A E E F R C U C A
I E T R R P O G N A M N
T N A R R U C D E R L A
E E H C Y L L E M O N B
```

RASPBERRY	ORANGE	LYCHEE
REDCURRANT	MANGO	CHERRY
BANANA	LEMON	KIWI
TANGERINE	APRICOT	GRAPE
STRAWBERRY	PEACH	PEAR
POMEGRANATE	MANDARIN	APPLE
BLACKCURRANT	NECTARINE	MELON

PLEASE TURN OVER FOR DETAILS ON HOW TO ENTER

HOW TO ENTER

All the words listed overleaf, below the word puzzle, are hidden in the grid. You can find them by reading the letters forward, backwards, up or down, or diagonally. When you find a word, circle it or put a line through it, the remaining letters (which you can read from left to right, from the top of the puzzle through to the bottom) will spell a secret message.

After you have filled in all the words, don't forget to fill in your name and address in the space provided and pop this page in an envelope (you don't need a stamp) and post it today. Hurry - competition ends December 31st. 1989.

Mills & Boon Competition,
FREEPOST,
P.O. Box 236,
Croydon,
Surrey. CR9 9EL
Only one entry per household

Secret Message _____

_____

Name _____

Address _____

_____

_____

_____ Postcode _____

You may be mailed as a result of entering this competition
Please tick the box if you are a Reader Service subscriber ☐

COMP7